WEREWOLF BODYGUARD

Big City Lycans
Book Four

New York Times and USA Today Bestselling Author

Eve Langlais

Copyright Werewolf Bodyguard © Eve Langlais 2022/2023

Cover Art © by Melony Paradise of ParadiseCoverDesign.com 2022

Produced in Canada

Published by Eve Langlais

http://www.EveLanglais.com

eBook: ISBN: 978 1 77384 380 3

Print ISBN: 978 1 77384 381 0

PROLOGUE

THE CRAMPED, dank cell they were kept in had no windows. No light. A good thing since they didn't have to see the moldy garbage given to them. Bits that crunched between the teeth, too sharp to swallow. Fuzz that didn't belong on whatever squishy lump they were fed.

A good thing survival didn't care about a best-before date. Quinn and his four friends—down from the seven captured, three having died of their injuries—lived day to day, not that they could mark the passing of time in this dark place.

After six such meals, the door opened—rather than the slot through which they tossed in the food—and Horace got dragged out by their masked captors. The enemy, according to the government and the military to which Quinn and his platoon belonged.

Horace didn't return. Neither did Jorge. Or Gunner. Or Brock. Until only Quinn remained.

When it was Quinn's turn, he fought, or tried to, lashing out at the men gripping his arms. Already weak from his imprisonment, his attempt to fight accomplished nothing, and so they dragged him into a stone chamber, one with a single window set high in the wall and covered in bars.

There was no furniture in the room, nothing but a dirty stone floor, stained in spots. Some of it was still damp, the blood spilled still fresh. He'd long lost his sense of smell given his lack of bathing, and yet his nose wrinkled at a strong musky odor that he realized emanated from a corner with a pile of rags—

Wait, that was a man. The figure lifted a head, the crown of it topped in a wild, tangled mane of hair that blended into the beard that covered most of the face. From that mess, piercing green eyes perused him.

One of his captors went to stand near the man and yelled something Quinn couldn't understand. The wild-haired guy kept staring at Quinn rather than pay attention. He earned a blow that rocked him and caused a metallic jingle. Only then did Quinn notice the chain that went from an embedded bolt in the wall to the collar around the prisoner's neck.

Was this another soldier? Hard to tell. But Quinn tried. "Who are you? What's going to happen?"

The queries earned him a cuff that caused him to bite his tongue. Coppery blood filled his mouth. To his disgust, his hungry body welcomed something other than the crap he'd been eating to survive.

More yelling ensued, along with another kick that

led to the ramshackle figure rising and shambling toward Quinn. It took a moment for him to realize he could hear a whisper. "Don't be afraid."

Afraid of what?

A sudden grip of both of his arms by his masked guards held him in place as the guy neared. A third fellow, the one who'd done the kicking, reached Quinn first and grabbed at his tattered sleeve, ripping it, and exposing his flesh.

What was happening?

The scarecrow stopped in front of him and muttered, "Don't fight it. This won't hurt for long."

The man had no weapon. Stick thin, he likely had little strength, and yet fear iced Quinn's veins. He uttered a startled yell as the scarecrow bent and bit his forearm!

"Fuck off." Quinn roared and struggled anew as those teeth clamped down and didn't let go. Skin broke. Blood flowed. Pain proved quick and surprisingly intense.

It took a cuff before the scarecrow released his flesh, leaving behind a perfect crescent bite that bled copiously and burned something fierce.

The scarecrow stared at him with those vivid green eyes, the apology in their depths at odds with the blood staining his beard and lips.

"What have you done to me?" Quinn exclaimed. While not one given to flights of fancy, he couldn't help but recall the last zombie movie he'd seen.

As the scarecrow shuffled back to this corner, chains clinking, he mumbled, "You'll either live or die."

A cryptic reply for Quinn to mull over later as he got dragged away and tossed into a new cell, one with a window too high to be of any use. Even if he could climb, the bars in it were too closely situated for him to squeeze through. But he did appreciate the light. It allowed him to see the damage done to his arm.

A bite mark. And a vicious one at that. Already the edges of it turned red and angry. It throbbed something fierce, but more worrisome was the feverish heat building in his body.

Holy fuck, I've been infected with something. With what? Most plagues were airborne or passed via fluids. A chomp that broke skin certainly fell into the latter.

Would he die quickly? Painfully? Would he survive? The scarecrow had said he'd either live or die. Given the situation, he had yet to decide which he preferred. Not entirely true. Given his young age, barely legal to drink, he would choose life. But what at what price would he earn it?

As the fever took hold, sweat oozed from his pores, wicking out what little moisture remained in his body. The thirst hit him next, his mouth so dry and parched, but the worst? The hunger. Such hunger that when he finally came to his senses, he crawled to the plate of disgusting food left for him, squirming with maggots and green mold, and stuffed it into his mouth.

He gagged and spat it out. Could have cried with frustration but yelled instead, hoarsely and not for long, as he passed out and endured the craziest dream, one where he had four legs and ran under a full moon.

When next he woke, he heard moaning and pressed his ear to the slot in his door for a listen.

"Fucking assholes. I'm gonna string you by your balls," a familiar voice yelled.

"Brock?" he said more in surprise than anything else. He'd thought his friend dead.

"Quinn, that you?"

"Yeah."

"Those assholes forced some dickwad to bite me!" Brock exclaimed.

"Me too." Then Quinn added, "Why?"

"I'm thinking it's the plague. They're infecting us on purpose."

"Why not just kill us?"

"Because I'll bet once they know we're carriers they release us to spread it!"

It sounded all too plausible, and Quinn knew it had long been a fear of the military. "If it was dangerous, shouldn't we be dead?" The rational voice joining the conversation took Quinn by surprise.

"Gunner? They got you too?" he queried.

"Not for long. I am getting out of here," Gunner said.

A goal Quinn approved of, even as it seemed impossible. There was no lock to pick on this side of the door. Thus far, his captors always came into the cell a pair or more at a time, making it an unfair fight.

"Did you recognize the guy they had bite us?" Quinn asked instead.

"No, but he's definitely not local," Gunner replied.

"Why they got him chained?" was Brock's query. "Didn't seem all that dangerous to me."

No, but at the same time, Quinn knew that even the most unlikely seeming could have super strength if adrenalized. Just ask any nurse who'd dealt with an emaciated drug user how strong they could be.

"Did you guys get the fever and shakes?" Quinn wondered aloud.

"Yeah," Gunner stated. "Weird dreams too."

"I think we all did." Brock's stark statement.

"What about Horace and Jorge? They in here too?" They'd been talking unimpeded through their slots, just the three of them.

"I don't know," Brock stated. "Although I did hear someone screaming the first day they put me in here."

Live or die. Those words echoed in his head. Were he, Gunner, and Brock the only ones left?

Outside his window, day waned and turned to night, the clouds blocking the stars and moon, making his cell gloomy. He dozed off, only to awake suddenly. Upon opening his eyes, he noticed he lay in a patch of moonlight.

Its light prickled the skin uncomfortably. He grimaced as he tried to shift out of its path. Only the tingle intensified and turned into a burning. His limbs throbbed and began to swell, but he didn't grunt until he heard the first crack.

As if he'd broken a bone.

Then another.

Sharp pain hit him, and he clutched his midsection with arms that didn't want to fold right.

What was happening?

He moaned as he writhed on the floor, his body contorting in agony, his gasps and grunts turning to huffs and...yips?

He went to push himself to his feet, only to realize he couldn't stand. Not on two legs at any rate since he appeared to have four. And paws.

What the fuck?

He went to yell, but it emerged as a bark.

A bark with a reply.

Yip. Snarl. Bark. Howl.

"*Awoo!*" He ululated his confusion.

The bite made sense now. They had been trying to infect him.

And succeeded.

I'm a fucking werewolf.

It might have been the most demoralizing moment, only the door to his cell suddenly clicked.

He eyed it and waited. It opened to show the scarecrow outside. A scarecrow standing tall, his eyes feverish bright, his beard covered in blood. Fresh blood.

The scarecrow whispered, "Time to run free, brothers." The man shambled off, and Quinn followed into the narrow corridor to see two other wolves peeking from their cells. Somehow, he could identify Brock from Gunner.

He uttered a sharp bark, and the scarecrow glanced over his shoulder. "I know you have questions. We don't have time. They'll soon realize I've escaped. Run the moment you get outside. Run and don't look back. And if you make it back to civilization, find a pack. They can explain everything."

The voice, rusty as if from disuse, spoke and made little sense other than the running part. Quinn wanted with every fiber of his being to race in the moonlight.

The scarecrow led the wolves to a door with a handle they wouldn't have been able to turn with paws. It opened to reveal two men with guns.

They yelled and fired. The scarecrow jerked as a bullet hit him in the chest, which led to him roaring and exploding into a massive werewolf. A frenzy of screams and gunfire ensued, but two soldiers were no match for the wolves. Quinn couldn't restrain his blood lust. His need to kill.

By the time the soldiers stopped moving, Quinn and the others all had red muzzles. But they should have kept one alive, given the door that now foiled their exit plan. Paws and handles didn't mix. Their escape might have ended there if someone hadn't opened it to check on their comrades.

Brock was the one to pounce while Quinn used his body to hold open the door that they might pass through. They found themselves outside in the compound of the rebel forces that had captured them. The full moon illuminated everything, including the trucks parked for the night. The back of one held dead bodies wrapped in dirty linen, already rotting. He'd found Jorge and Horace. Killed by the bite.

No. Killed by their captors who did this to them.

Despite not being able to speak in words, he and the others appeared to be of one mind. Their sense of smell partially guided them, but instinct also played a part as their desire for vengeance led them to the enemies that kept them prisoner.

They showed no mercy. The hunger wouldn't allow it. While the meat tempted, they didn't linger once the killing was done. They ran as instructed, only to slow to match the limping scarecrow's pace. Even as a wolf he appeared gaunt and ill fed.

They made it to the foothills where they could disappear should any of their captors choose to chase them. They kept moving until Scarecrow collapsed. Quinn and the others could have left him behind, but instead they lay down around the man who'd released them from their prison. The one with answers to their questions.

And Quinn had so many.

Despite not meaning to, Quinn slept and didn't wake until the dawn, naked but in his own body again. All of them were, even Scarecrow, who breathed shallowly.

It was Brock who found a stream with water. They carried Scarecrow to it and did their best to drip some between his parched lips.

The man had a fever, most likely due to the seven

bullet wounds riddling his flesh. They didn't bleed, but their angry edges and leaking pus didn't bode well.

Scarecrow regained consciousness enough to say, "I'm dying. Leave me. Go home."

"Easier said than done," grumbled Brock.

"What did you do to us?" asked Gunner.

Scarecrow turned his head to offer a sad smile. "Made you special. You're all Lycan now."

"You mean werewolves." A bitter retort by Quinn.

"Yes."

"How do we get rid of it?" Gunner really didn't sound happy.

"You can't." Scarecrow coughed, and blood frothed his lips. "You are Lycan for life. Find a pack. Most major cities have one. They can explain."

"Explain what?" Quinn asked.

"Everything. But most important, sire no babies. Tell no one. Bewa—" The word hissed into silence as Scarecrow passed out. He didn't wake, and his breathing grew shallower.

"Fuck me, what should we do?" Gunner muttered.

"Leave," an agitated and pacing Brock declared.

"To go where?" Quinn retorted.

"Somewhere with fucking pants for starters." Brock glared down at his swinging dick as if blaming it for their lack of clothes.

"We can't leave. He's still alive." Gunner pointed to Scarecrow, almost a corpse, his breathing so shallow it barely moved his chest.

"Not for long. And we'll join him if we don't find food and shelter," Quinn pointed out.

In the end, they left, having placed Scarecrow in the vee of some rocks, his body limp and so feverish it was a wonder he didn't combust.

The next few days were a blur, staggering with no real clear direction, parched and starving. Naked, their skin burned by the sun. Yet, somehow, they survived and, in a stroke of luck, ran into a military patrol who was shocked to find them alive.

They'd already discussed beforehand that they should keep their werewolf thing secret, Scarecrow's warning not needed since they knew what would happen if it was discovered. Brock said it best, *"We'll be guinea wolves in a cage getting poked the rest of our lives."* Because the Lycan thing wasn't a fluke or a one-time thing. When exposed to the full moon, they changed. Meaning they did their best to stay hidden out of sight on those nights.

It wasn't hard for them to get a doctor to declare them suffering from PTSD after their ordeal. They got shipped back Stateside, and Gunner immediately took off. Brock stuck with Quinn a while before going his own way.

Only Quinn sought to do what Scarecrow said. He went back to Canada, found a pack, and learned what it meant to be a Lycan.

1

MANY YEARS LATER...

We have a job for you. The message arrived via a secured channel that only Quinn could access. The missive continued. *You are to accompany Dr. Silver and guard her from harm.* It didn't say from who. *Tell no one where you're going, or why. Not even your alpha.*

Meaning this mission was a secret one. The Cabal, those governing werewolf affairs, did enjoy their cloak-and-dagger games. A good thing his pack alpha proved understanding about Quinn flitting off with little notice. All it took was for him to say, "I got a special job," and Gavin, his friend and leader, gave him the go-ahead to leave.

But, this time, Quinn balked, and for more than one reason. One, he'd already spent too much time in the company of the irritable Dr. Silver. Two, he'd barely been home, and his plastic plants were looking dusty. And three, he didn't want to travel with her.

Something about Dr. Erryn Silver drew him, and it was more than her looks. She had striking features: short hair that wisped, the tips frosted, her eyes more golden yellow than brown, and a trim, athletic figure. The scars he'd seen on her arms from a werewolf attack in her early twenties didn't bother him, although he did wonder how far they extended. Not that he'd asked and this despite his curiosity that she'd not only recovered from a werewolf attack while at university but then somehow got roped in by the Cabal to work for them.

It baffled Quinn on a few levels, the first being how anyone severely scarred and most likely traumatized by the Lycan would want to work for them. After all, it wasn't as if she could be turned. Only men could be bitten and become werewolves.

Secondly, why did the Cabal make an exception for her? Usually those who found out Lycans existed were handled in one of two ways. The Cabal either ensured the person making the claim come off as unhinged, making it appear they were using drugs and hallucinating—easy today with all the stuff available. For those who persisted and tried to expose the Lycan secret? They simply disappeared—aka died.

Silver hadn't been killed or ridiculed. Instead, the Cabal chose to hire her and let her dig into the Lycan secrets they'd been keeping for centuries. Why? And what of Silver's motive? What did she hope to accomplish? It wasn't as if she could publish her findings.

Not his business. His only concern should be the

mission. A hard thing to remember when forced to be around the sexy woman. Thank fuck her scent repulsed. He couldn't have said why exactly, but she didn't smell right. It didn't help she doused herself in a strong perfume each day. She lacked any kind of taste, given the odors she chose clashed. For example, her most recent mix of coconut, cinnamon, and lavender.

Did the doctor not have a sense of smell? She certainly lacked a pleasant attitude. At least around him. It appeared they reciprocated their dislike of each other. She had nothing but disdain and scowls for Quinn. Acted as if he were beneath her. Hoity-toity human. This trip they'd be embarking upon together should be fun.

Quinn waited outside the house where recently married—and new parents—Honey and Ulric currently resided. A house across the street from her parents so they could help the young couple out. That they even had a child was a miracle, given Ulric was Lycan. Usually such a pregnancy would have killed the mother, but with Dr. Silver's aide, both mother and child survived. Daily vitamin shots and a sealed room that ensured not a single sliver of the full moon penetrated had somehow kept Ulric's mate alive.

The question that everyone had? Was the baby a werewolf? A full moon had gone by without any sign of the child going furry. By the end of a second, the doctor felt ready to move on. And lucky Quinn, he'd been ordered to go with her.

He'd already said his goodbyes, which were brief.

To Dorian, "Watch my place, would you?" To Ulric, "Enjoy the shitty diapers." And to his alpha, Griffin, "Sorry to leave you in the lurch," to which his boss and friend replied, "When the Cabal calls, you have to answer."

As to the mission, when he'd called Silver to make arrangements for their trip, he'd asked, "What are we looking for?"

"Lycan babies."

"You're fucking joking, right?"

While the doctor appeared convinced others existed, Quinn didn't share that belief. He'd seen what she'd done to keep just one alive. *Vitamins my ass.* He knew there had to be more in those needles than just some extra nutrients. Others caught in that situation would not have had the same kind of one-on-one attention and medicine. Meaning Quinn thought this was a stupid quest, but one did not say no to the Cabal. Not after they saved his life after his return to Canada from abroad.

Bewildered by his new Lycan side, he'd almost been shot the first time he shifted on a full moon. Hunters in Ontario didn't like wolves near the suburbs. Luckily, he ran into Griffin—the leader of the Ottawa Byward Pack—in the woods. The man had been forced to report Quinn's existence to the Cabal. Once they heard he had military training, well, let's just say they had uses for a man of his skills.

Skills that now involved babysitting a stubborn doctor.

Silver emerged from the house with only a single suitcase, which surprised. Most woman traveled with enough changes of clothing to last them through every kind of weather condition. She had a laptop bag slung over her shoulder, no purse.

She didn't smile upon seeing him leaning against the SUV that would take them to the airport. So he offered her the biggest, shit-eating grin and a drawled, "What's up, Doc?"

The glare was totally worth it.

Ulric stood in a second-floor window with the baby in the crook of his arm. He waved. They'd already said their goodbyes. Most likely Honey was napping. She'd also hugged him earlier and thanked him for all he'd done. Whatever. Ulric was pack. Which made him a brother. Which made her and the baby Quinn's family too.

The trunk to the SUV remained open as Silver loaded her own stuff. He'd learned early on to not offer her aide. She had an independent streak.

The passenger door slammed shut as she joined him. The close confines of the SUV meant he had to breathe in her obnoxious scent. The cool weather meant he couldn't crack his window to minimize it. Nor could he put on an N95 from the leftover stash in his glove box from when they had the Covid regulations mandating their use. At least she didn't talk. She pulled out her laptop and worked.

She worked in the airport once they passed security. She worked on the private jet the Cabal arranged, the plush seats giving him enough room to stretch a bit and catch a nap. They landed outside London at a smaller airport than Heathrow. They were supposed to simply refuel and take off again, only the captain emerged from the cockpit, sweating and pale.

"Sorry, folks. Not feeling too hot. Gonna have to bail, but I placed a call, and someone is on their way to replace me."

Given that would be a few hours, Quinn and Silver disembarked and entered the dinky terminal in search of a hot meal. He'd not eaten anything other than peanuts since they'd taken off. They didn't have an attendant for their trip, as they'd chosen to go ahead and fend for themselves.

They overpaid for some bland meal before returning to their jet as twilight fell. It had been refueled and awaited its new pilot, who'd supposedly arrived but was going through security.

As they boarded, his nose twitched. Something didn't smell right.

"What's wrong?" Silver actually spoke to him.

"Someone's been on the plane."

She glanced around. "Most likely the customs officials looking for contraband."

Her excuse made sense. Still...

He eyed the back of the plane and the hatch in the floor to the tight storage space. He rose and headed for it just as footsteps hit the stairs onto the jet. A glance over his shoulder showed a man boarding, wearing a uniform and a cap. Their new pilot had arrived.

"Evening," said the man with the deep voice. "Captain Jameson." He held out his hand and provided a firm shake. His scent entirely normal, if human.

Silver went straight to business. "How soon can we depart?"

"Right away. I've already gotten clearance for a runway if we can get this baby going in the next few minutes. So unless we're waiting for someone else?" The captain glanced past them, probably looking for an attendant.

"It's just us."

"Then let's be on our way." The captain pulled the door shut and headed into the cockpit. He didn't lock the door Quinn noticed, a trusting guy.

The engines of the plane soon hummed, and Silver seated herself, but he glanced at the hatch in the floor providing access to their luggage. Maybe just a quick peek. He rose from his seat.

"What are you doing?" Silver asked.

"Checking something." It took only a few strides to reach the rear. He crouched and lifted the hatch for a look, the loud rumble of the motors masking Silver's steps as she neared and stood over him.

"What's wrong?"

"Possibly nothing." He leaned down to look in the hole, saw their bags, the same ones he'd loaded hours before. But the scent among them? Definitely new. Could be airport customs officials.

19

The plane jolted as it began moving, heading for a runway. They'd be taking off in a minute.

The nagging in his gut persisted. He reached into the cargo hold and pulled out his duffel bag. The weight of it felt right, the zipper still locked shut. He couldn't stop customs officers from opening it, but it would deter casual thieves. He pulled out Silver's suitcase next and paused.

"You found something." Stated not asked.

"Your luggage is heavier." Which seemed odd given it too remained locked. "And someone touched it." He could smell the leather of gloves on it and something else.

"Are you sure?"

"Yeah." What did it mean? Had someone planted contraband in her luggage?

Silver pursed her lips. "I don't like it."

For once they agreed. "Whatever it is, I can pull it out before we land."

"But it will still be on board." The plane was moving steadily. Soon they'd be on their runway, picking up speed.

"Maybe we can flush it when we're in the air?" he suggested.

"I have a better idea. Let's go," she commanded, moving from him to snare her laptop and slide it back in her bag.

"What?"

"We're getting off this flight."

"Seriously?"

"What's your gut say?"

He didn't hesitate. "There's something wrong."

"I agree. So open that door."

"We're about to take off."

"Then stop arguing." She slipped on her jacket and zipped it. He slung his duffel onto his shoulder, but when he would have grabbed her suitcase, she shook her head. "Leave it."

"If you say so." She was in charge on this trip. Not to mention it was her shit they'd be abandoning. He cranked the wheel to the door. It unsealed with a hiss. He eyed the cockpit. The captain would have noticed, and yet he didn't emerge or act.

The plane picked up speed. Soon they'd be stuck.

He shoved open the door and wind tugged at them.

Silver didn't hesitate; she jumped.

Jeezus!

He didn't think but dove after her, legs pedaling in the air, and then jolting as one foot then the other hit the ground hard. He stumbled a few paces, off balance due to his duffel. To his surprise Silver remained on her feet and seemed unharmed, her expression as blank as usual.

The plane they'd just escaped lifted into the air, the door gaping wide. At a few hundred feet, it exploded!

21

2

"Run," Erryn yelled the moment burning pieces of the exploded plane began to fall.

Self-preservation kicked in, and Quinn needed no prompting.

Together, they raced for the perimeter of the airport, not wanting to be seen. After all, someone had just tried to eliminate them. Whatever caused the explosion wasn't an accident. If it hadn't been for Quinn's instinct, they would be barbecued meat. Instead, Erryn had no clothes, just the laptop, which she'd saved, and her wallet.

The chain link fence provided handholds for her to haul herself up. The barbed wire crowning it proved a little more difficult, but a quick-thinking Quinn stripped his sweater off and threw it over the sharp tines, giving them a spot to cross over without shredding skin. He pulled it free once they'd both leaped to safety on the other side.

Behind them sirens blared as emergency vehicles came flying to the rescue, not that there was much left to save. Erryn, crouched alongside Quinn, watched as the first of the vehicles reached the wreckage of the burning Cessna. A wing here. A chunk of the tail there.

"Someone tried to kill us," Quinn stated, not in surprise but matter of fact.

"Could have been an accident," she countered to be contrary.

He snorted. "I might not be well versed in aviation, but even I know planes don't explode that spectacularly without some help."

"So who did you piss off?" Because while people didn't like Silver, no one currently hated her. Not that she knew of.

"Me?" He snorted. "That's hilarious coming from Doctor Charming. Maybe someone doesn't want you completing this mission."

"The Cabal is the one who gave me permission. If they didn't want me seeking out Lycan babies, they would have said no."

"Who says it's all of them? Only takes one to blow shit up." A reminder they'd recently had an issue with a crooked Cabal member.

She frowned. "I guess it's possible." While she was familiar with most of them, she couldn't vouch for their states of mind, especially on such a forbidden subject as Lycan pregnancy.

Quinn muttered, "I don't see anyone in the area that isn't wearing an airport uniform."

She'd been checking the people arriving as well. Whoever tried to kill them might have stuck around to ensure the job got done. "They could be at a distance using binoculars." Meaning they might not have escaped without notice.

He grimaced. "Yeah." He glanced over his shoulder as if he could see anyone targeting them in the dark. "Although I'm pretty sure someone who came prepared with a bomb probably has a rifle and would have shot us while we were vulnerable on the fence."

"Not if they wanted this to appear like an accident," she countered.

"Whatever the case, we shouldn't stick around." No need for him to say in case they tried again.

As they trudged away from the scene of chaos, she murmured, "I can hook you up with some people who can help you get back home." This deadly attack gave her the opportunity to ditch Quinn. She'd never wanted to be saddled with a bodyguard in the first place.

"Leave, as in without you?"

"I'll be fine. I'm used to taking care of myself."

"I'm sure you are," he replied flatly. "But I'm not leaving. Th Cabal ordered me to protect you."

She frowned. "And you did. I'm alive."

"For now. If this was targeted, then once they realize they fucked up, they'll try again."

"You're assuming they'll find me."

"If the Cabal has a traitor, then the moment you check in, they'll come after you again," Quinn argued.

"You're assuming it's them. Could be their enemies were sending a message. After all, it wouldn't be that hard for them to track a Cabal-owned jet. It wasn't as if our flight path was a secret. Not to mention, anyone could have followed us to the airport."

"Next you'll be saying maybe it was a spark in the fuel tank," he drawled sarcastically.

"We don't know for sure it was a bomb." It seemed most likely, but again, she liked antagonizing him.

"Why else would your suitcase change weight?"

"Maybe you just thought it did."

"Jeezus you're contrary. Why me?" he groaned to the sky.

"If you don't like it, go home. You have my blessing. Just do me a favor. If anyone asks, I died in the blast."

"My mission is to protect you."

"And you failed," was her brutal reply. Because if being nice wouldn't work, maybe being insulting would. In her experience, men couldn't handle criticism.

"How did I fail? You're still alive."

"No thanks to you. I was the one who said we should get off the plane."

"Only because I listened to my gut and found your luggage tampered with. If not for me, you would have blown up on that plane."

Annoyed at the truth, she pursed her lips. "It will be easier for me to travel alone."

"How do you figure that? You're a woman by herself in Europe. You'll be noticed."

"You do realize in this day and age women travel by themselves."

"Doesn't mean it's not dangerous."

"I don't need a man to protect me," she snapped as they reached a road and began walking along its shoulder.

"Apparently, you do, seeing as how your plan to be a martyr is dumb."

"Who says I'm trying to die?"

"What is your plan then? Because, in case you hadn't noticed, we can't exactly fly unless you want to let the killer know we survived."

"Why fly when I can travel by train? And before you open your mouth and say anything about tracking, I can pay cash." She patted her hip where she'd stashed a wad. She never trusted everything to bags.

"Ah yes, because whipping out a large sum in cash won't get noticed."

"You have a better idea?"

"We drive. I know where to get us a car."

"There is no we. I told you, go home."

His lips flattened. "I am not disobeying a Cabal order."

"I am trying to save your life."

"I'm supposed to be looking after yours," he growled in reply.

"And you did. I'm alive. Congrats. Job well done."

He scowled. "Ain't gonna work, Doc. I'm sticking with you."

She should have known he'd be stubborn. "Fine." She sulked, only a little. In reality, it was nice to not be walking by herself on this dark, lonely stretch of road. Especially when a transport truck stopped to offer a ride. He took one look at Quinn and wisely didn't make any moves that would have necessitated Erryn taking action.

She wasn't being facetious when she claimed she could handle most threats. She'd been protecting herself for a long time. Her mother died her first year of university, and she never knew her father.

The truck driver dropped them off at a highway exit whose name meant nothing to her, but Quinn appeared to know where he wanted to go. He led them through a warren of connected alleys that had her completely lost and cringing at the smell. Urine had a tendency of clinging to stone and getting worse when things got rained on and damp. Which described London pretty much most of the time. Or so she'd heard. She'd never actually spent much time here. Too big of a city. Erryn never did like crowds.

Quinn stopped by a door that didn't have any markings on it. A sharp rap followed by two, then one, then three and a pause resulted in it being unbolted and opened.

The guy who opened it took one look at Quinn and grinned. "When did you get into town?"

"Hey, Brock." Quinn shook the proffered hand that dragged him into a back-slapping hug.

When Brock released him, he turned an engaging smile on her next. "And who is this? Did you get married and not invite me?"

"We're not a couple," Quinn hastily replied.

"Not even close. I'm Ryn." She offered an abbreviation of her name.

"Ryn. Such a lovely name for a beautiful, single lady." Brock arched a brow as he fished.

She snorted, not taken in by his charm. She'd met and rejected slicker. "Single, yes. Looking, no."

"I wouldn't mess with her," Quinn retorted, entering the building. "She's Cabal."

"Quinn!" She couldn't help a shocked exhalation of his name.

Quinn snorted. "Don't get your panties in a twist, Doc. You can trust Brock. Known him a while. We used to serve together. Were, turned by the same guy." Making Brock a werewolf.

A werewolf in London?

She arched a brow as she stepped past Brock to also enter. "I thought London didn't have an official pack." They'd run into territory issues with a very old vampire flock. Only one pack remained in the UK, located in Wales.

"I'm what you call a special exception," Brock declared, closing the door firmly behind them and sliding a bar across.

It turned out to be a garage slash apartment. The

main floor had a bay door with a few vehicles parked, one of them up on a lift. Tools lay scattered around, along with toolchests on wheels to organize them. The stairs led to an open loft living space. A tiny kitchen area was comprised of a counter, fridge, mini stove, and sink. No kitchen table, just a narrow butcher block island with a pair of stools. There was a couch that dipped in the middle and a chair that looked equally lived in. The bed platform appeared to be wooden skids with a mattress and a jumbled comforter on top.

Definite bachelor pad.

"What are you doing in London?" Brock asked, heading for the fridge and pulling out a few beers.

"Was only supposed to be a stopover, but we had plane issues."

Brock froze midturn, and his jaw dropped. "Fuck me, you were on that Cessna that blew up!"

"Not actually in it or we wouldn't be talking," Quinn quipped, grabbing the proffered bottle.

Erryn took one to be polite but didn't plan to drink. She never did. Losing control wasn't an option. Not for her. Not ever.

After taking a swig, Quinn asked, "What are they saying about it?"

"That it was a spark in the fuel system, which sounded like bullshit because, how the fuck does a tank spark after a plane's taken off?" Brock scoffed.

"It was a bomb in the luggage compartment."

Brock uttered a low whistle. "Who did you piss off?"

Rather than correct the assumption, Erryn let Quinn's friend think it was about him.

"What have you heard about the passengers and crew?" Quinn continued to question his friend.

"Reports said there were three people on board. No survivors and no names released."

"Good. And in case it wasn't clear, we'd like to keep it that way."

"No one will hear you're alive from me, although once they sift the wreckage and don't find your bodies, they'll know you're alive," Brock pointed out.

"By then we should be long gone, which is why we're here. I need some wheels that won't draw attention."

The right thing to demand, and yet Erryn's gaze kept straying to the bright blue convertible.

Brock caught her. "She's a beauty, ain't she? Belongs to a vampire princess. Spoiled brat but her daddy pays me well to deal with her highness."

"Got anything that won't get us hunted by vampires and targeted by car jackers?" Quinn drawled.

"Not here I don't, but if you can wait until morning, I can get the keys to a few options."

Quinn glanced at Erryn. "Mind waiting a few hours?"

A part of her wanted to be unreasonable and say, *Not here.* There was nowhere to be alone other than the walled-off corner that she imagined held a bathroom. One bed. One lumpy couch. It wouldn't be a restful night. She could always sleep in the car tomorrow.

"Sure."

"I got clean towels and shit if you wanna shower or something," Brock offered.

She almost said no, and then sanity kicked in. First rule of survival? Recharge when you got a chance. "That would be great. Thanks."

She took her laptop bag into the surprisingly clean bathroom. The walls only went eight feet, the height of the drywall. The ceiling slanted overhead another four feet or so, and had it been day, she'd have not needed to flick a switch, given the skylight would provide plenty of illumination. And hopefully no Peeping Toms.

She turned on the water in the shower before making a phone call via a secured channel. The line answered, but no one spoke. She couldn't blame them, given the number calling belonged to someone supposedly dead.

"It's me. I'm alive." No need to say anything more. They knew each other well enough to recognize the other.

While Cabal, her mentor Fred, the man who'd saved her many, many years ago, would never betray her.

A sigh sounded. "Thank god."

"Thank Quinn." She kept her tone low lest she be heard over the shower. "His wolfy sense let us know our shit was tampered with."

"He noticed it before you?" Not quite mockery and

yet she grimaced because it did burn that he'd been the one to realize it first.

"They put something in my bag. Either a bomb on a timer or pressure activated." Which would have triggered once the plane got to a certain height. "Once we realized we'd been tagged, we got off the plane."

"Sounds like it was close."

She didn't mention it was literally a matter of seconds. A minute more, they'd both be dead. "Important thing is they failed. They think I'm dead."

"If this is about the mission—"

"Then it means we're on the right track." And someone wasn't happy about it. Not completely unexpected and something she and Fred had discussed at length before she'd dared to embark on this quest.

"Is it worth it, though? They tried to kill you. Maybe we should call it off."

"No!" A hasty reply. "The packs deserve to know the truth."

The truth being that Lycans could have babies under certain circumstances. It didn't have to be catastrophic for the mother and child. But there were some that preferred to stick to the old ways. Either sterilize before they were changed or immediately after. No exception. Those who wished to have children had to do so before an alpha bit them to see if they could become Lycan. Once they turned, their only other recourse was to adopt. Sadly, and thankfully at once, there was no shortage of orphaned boys in need of a home. By the time they were adults, Lycans in their lives could usually figure out who would make a good packmate.

But one nagging question remained, who created the first Lycan? It was the chicken-and-the-egg conundrum.

"What does Quinn think of your objective?"

"Honestly? We've not spoken much of it."

"He's always been discreet. Does his job well and without drama."

"Are you calling me dramatic?"

Her mentor coughed. "Never. Which isn't a good thing. You could use a bit of chaos to shake you up."

"You think I haven't lived through enough?" was her sarcastic retort.

"I think that you thrive when you're challenged."

She grimaced because she hated to agree.

"Where are you now?" Fred asked.

"Somewhere safe. I hope. We're with an old army buddy of Quinn's. We should be on the road in the morning."

"You've told him about the mission?" he asked sharply.

"Of course not." She could only hope that was true. After all, she'd left Quinn alone with his friend. Who knew what they chatted about. "But speaking of, I should get back to them."

"Yes. But first let me add, you can trust Quinn."

"How can you be sure?"

"Because."

"That's a terrible answer."

33

"I know."

She wanted to sigh, but at the same time, she'd trusted this man for more than decade. "I still don't know why you sent him with me. I can take care of myself."

"As if I'd let you do this alone. Our mistake was trying to be open and honest about your quest," her mentor grumbled. "Should have kept it a secret and just presented the results."

"Secrets have a tendency of outing themselves," she reminded him as she started to strip. She'd have to shower quick to cover the time spent speaking.

"And some secrets have people who are willing to kill to keep them."

"Speaking of secrets, don't tell anyone you talked to me. As far as anyone knows, Quinn and I died in the explosion." She felt a twinge saying it knowing how close Quinn was to his Pack.

"I already figured as much." A pause then a soft, "You don't have to do this, Ryn. You can come home."

Actually, she did have to, and Fred knew it. "I'll call you when we get to our next destination." She wasn't about to give up now.

"Be careful."

"I'll do my best." Because her life depended on it.

3

THE WATER WENT on in the tiny bathroom, creating a muffling effect. Just in case, Quinn dragged Brock down the stairs to the business side of the garage for a whispered conversation.

"What do you know?" Quinn asked without preamble.

Brock's jaw tensed before he sighed. "I should have known you'd see right through me. So, while the human authorities think you died on that plane, the vampires are aware you didn't."

"Why would vampires have been watching us? Were they involved?"

"They didn't plant the bomb; however they did have someone keeping an eye given a Cabal plane was on their turf."

"Since when does Lord Augustus trouble himself about transient visitors?" Quinn knew exactly who ruled the flock in these parts.

"He doesn't usually, but a jet landed with two Cabal agents. No warning or reason offered, and since there've been problems..."

"What kind of problems?"

Brock raked a hand through his hair. "The kind creating crimes scenes with a scent unlike anything I've ever encountered."

"You can't leave me dangling. What kind of crimes?"

"People are being killed. More specifically, vampires. Only young ones so far."

"How?"

Brock swiped a hand over his throat. "Slashed deep in the neck and then the heads basically twisted off."

"So they can't rise again." People made the mistake of thinking you could stake a vampire in the heart to kill them or just jab them with wood and poof. The only surefire way to kill a vampire? Decapitation. Even being burned by sunlight could be healed. With the older ones, it would take the body hours in direct UV rays before it crisped to the point of no return.

"Needless to say, having young'uns killed willy-nilly has the flock on edge."

"No shit. Any idea who's doing it?"

Brock shrugged. "Nope, but it's got them antsy."

"Do they think it's a Lycan?"

Brock nodded. "In their defense, I'd have to say it's very possible, given the neck slashes appear to have been done by claws."

"But why would the Lycans attack the vampires

like that?" Quinn's understanding was the packs in the UK were outnumbered by the vamps. It would be a massacre to antagonize them.

"That's the thing; it makes no sense. And I've tried telling them that, but as the body count rises, so does their paranoia. Some are starting to whisper it's a coup by the Lycans and it needs to be stopped. Permanently."

"Wiping out a pack would cause the rest to rise up," Quinn noted.

"Which would then draw in other agitated flocks."

Quinn's turn to whistle. "If that happens, we'll have a full-out war." And that would be hard to hide from humans in the digital age.

"Now you see."

"Are you safe?" Quinn asked. "Because if you need a place to go while shit blows over, my place is yours."

"Bah. I'm not worried. Augustus isn't listening to the idiots. Not yet at any rate."

"But if he does…"

"Then I will gladly squat at your place." Brock slapped him on the arm. "Much appreciated."

"Us grunts gotta stick together."

"Speaking of together, heard from Gunner lately?"

The reminder of his old friend had Quinn shaking his head. "Not in years." Gunner hadn't adapted to the change that well. The last time he'd seen him, the man had appeared strung out, his eyes wild, his skin feverish hot as if he fought through the Lycan infection still.

"I hope he found peace." Brock had been quickest

to accept the change and adapt. Quinn struggled only until he met Griffin. The man showed him a path forward.

"Me too, brother."

"So who's the woman?" Brock jerked his head in the direction of the second level.

"Client. Bodyguard stint."

Brock thought Quinn hired his services out as a mercenary, meaning bodyguard was an easy sell and not much of a lie.

"What does she need guarding from?"

"People who want to kill her apparently."

"Wait, the bomb on the plane, that was for your companion?" Brock ogled him.

"Most likely."

"Why? Who is she?"

"Someone who might blow apart some long-held lies." Quinn had never had an interest in children. Getting the big snip? Not a big deal. It meant not worrying about birth control. And a clean bill of health presented to a partner meant no rubber in the way. But some people actually wanted to fire live missiles and make babies. If it turned out the Lycan could breed? There'd be a lot of pissed-off dudes in the world.

Not that he told Brock any of that. He trusted his army friend, but he'd given his word he'd keep quiet. The one thing he did owe his friend? "You'll want to keep our visit a secret. I'm not sure how hardcore the folks going after her are. I don't want you to become collateral damage."

Brock rolled his eyes. "Holy fuck. Look at you, getting all emotional. I'll be fine. We both know I'm tough. Who dragged your ass out of those mountains?"

"Gunner dragged us both," he retorted. But Brock had been helping before that. Quinn's strength had failed first as they trudged their way back to camp. A good thing a patrol found them, or they'd have probably collapsed and died.

"I miss him, even if he is an ornery bastard."

"Me too." They'd been through something intense together. It felt wrong at times to be so far apart.

"Where you going next?"

"Can't say."

"You don't trust me?"

"More like I don't know. The lady tells me everything last second. Makes it hard to plan."

"Surprised you agreed to the job. Must pay well."

How to admit the Cabal didn't really give him much other than a congrats on a job well done? So why did he do this again? "Not really."

"Then it must be something else." Brock's gaze lifted to the second floor and the steam that rose from the enclosed bathroom to fog the skylight. A good thing or they might have seen a reflection they shouldn't.

The lights in the place flickered.

Brock glanced overhead and frowned. "Fucking pigeons."

"Say what?" Because that made no sense.

"With all the climate bullshit, brownouts and whatnot, I took this place off grid and went solar. Since there's no basement, I had to put the batteries and stuff on the roof, and no matter how I try to stop them, the pigeons manage to find a way to roost on my equipment. Oh, and they shit. Holy fuck, do they shit."

Quinn bit back a smile. "I hear they taste like chicken."

"A lie. They are tough, stringy bastards."

"Speaking of food, can we order in some pizza or something?" Quinn's tummy reminded him it had been a while since their airport meal.

"Fuck yeah. I know a place that makes a deep dish to put the Chicago ones to shame. Let me dig out their flyer." Brock headed for a workbench strewn with paper and a computer that looked outdated by a decade.

Quinn didn't point out the inanity of looking for a piece of paper when he could just as easily find the menu online. He headed upstairs to the living area, only to pause.

A scent tickled him. Roused him. Had him looking left and right before zeroing his gaze in on the bathroom.

It couldn't be Silver. She had that obnoxious smell about her. Maybe Brock had a girlfriend, and he'd caught a lingering whiff.

The door to the bathroom opened, and Silver emerged, hair damp from her shower, skin dewy, clothes the same as before. With her appearance, the nice scent disappeared, overpowered by something lemony mixed with pine. Gross.

She brought out her bag with her. An odd choice to bring into a place with water, given it carried her laptop. Then again, it also seemed to serve as her purse, and women kept all kinds of shit in those.

"Feeling more human?" he quipped.

"Never," was her deadpan reply.

Thunk. Her head tilted, and she looked upward. Her gaze narrowed. "What's above us?"

"Just the pigeons," Brock declared as he joined them, flyer in hand.

Thump. The hard knock vibrated.

"That ain't no pigeon," Quinn drawled.

Rather than reply, Brock reached down into his couch, and his hand re-emerged holding a shotgun. It made Quinn wish he had a piece, but he knew better than to bring one on a plane. It was easier to find one when he got to this destination. As if reading his mind, Brock jerked his head. "Kitchen island. There's a revolver."

Sweet. Quinn found it and flipped off the safety as Silver asked questions. "I take it it's unusual for there to be people on your roof?"

"Yeah. It ain't exactly nice what with the bird shit all over."

"No cameras?" asked Quinn.

"Not allowed on account of who I work for. The flock is camera shy."

"Could it be them?" he asked, eyeing the roof then the lower level. Silver saw his glance and nodded. Best to give themselves a space they didn't have to worry falling from.

Brock followed, his gaze on the skylight as they moved to the stairs. "I haven't done anything to warrant that type of visit, but then again, I'm also, as some would say, just a dumb dog."

"Nice partners," Silver replied dryly.

"I've called them worse behind their backs."

"Why do the vampires hate Lycans so much?" Silver asked.

"Know a lot of humans who can decapitate a person?" Brock countered.

"That can't be the only reason," she insisted.

Quinn snorted. "It's not. We also taste really bad, as do those we're close to."

"Interesting," was her muttered reply.

Bang. Bang. The skylight glass rattled but held.

For now.

"Could be a raccoon?" Brock suggested.

"Or we were followed." Quinn's grimmer reply.

"Whatever it is, won't be long before they get in," she observed. "We should leave."

"You guys go. I'm going to greet whatever the fuck is up there with some lead." Brock dug into his pocket and tossed them some keys. The emblem on them indicated they belonged to the Audi R8, the sweet blue convertible capable of a powerful six hundred horsepower.

"I thought that car belonged to that vampire princess," Quinn stated.

"Technically, she's a lady, and, yes, it does, so try to not break it."

"Won't she be pissed?" he asked.

"Very, but it's also the only one in the shop currently running." *Crack.* The glass overhead finally spiderwebbed. "Better get going."

"We're not leaving without you." As if Quinn would run.

Brock rolled his eyes. "For fuck's sake. Go. I'll be—"

The roof shuddered. Actually, the whole building did, as something took to pummeling the webbed glass until it fell in tinkling shards. A big body came hurtling down, a nightmare of teeth, fur, claws, and red eyes but looking rather humanoid standing on two legs, with two arms and a face that might just give Quinn nightmares.

"What the fuck is that?" Silver breathed as the thing launched itself for the stairs, the stunted wings at its back fluttering as it leaped and soared to hit the floor.

Brock had a better idea than questioning its origin. He shot it. *Bang. Bang. Bang.* Three good chest shots.

The creature looked down at the bleeding holes, which healed in seconds.

"Oh fuck," Brock muttered.

"Head shots only," Silver advised as she dug into her laptop bag.

Easier said than done.

Quinn aimed and fired, but the beast dodged the

bullet it moved so fucking fast. It hissed at them, its fang-like teeth slavering drool.

Before Quinn could shoot again, it lunged and slapped the barrel aside. Quinn managed to retain his grip and use it as a buffer from the claws that wanted to tear him apart.

Silver suddenly ran into the mix, arm raised, and plunged a needle that the monster didn't seem to give a shit about at first. Until its eyelids drooped. Then it turned to snarl, even as it wavered on its feet.

"Kill it," Silver yelled, backing away, holding its attention.

Quinn raised the revolver to shoot, but Brock fired first. A perfect head shot, through and through. The creature kept walking in Silver's direction.

Quinn's turn to fire. He took out a chunk of the skull, but it wouldn't go down. And then his gun fucking jammed!

Fuck it. Quinn waded in and swung the weapon, connecting with the head and doing even more damage. But the monster appeared intent on going after Doc.

"Fucker. That should have taken down an elephant," she cursed.

Bang. Bang. Brock stood close and kept firing until he ran out of bullets. When the creature wavered on its feet, Brock jumped on its back and grabbed hold of its head to twist.

Grasping his intent, Quinn did his best to help by

grabbing an arm. Doc snared the other, and they hung off them while Brock heaved and grunted.

Snap. Squish. Tear.

Gross.

The blood that poured from the stump was more black than red. It had a putrid stench too. The headless body wandered for a second before hitting a car and toppling over into the blue convertible, where it bled out and died.

Brock sighed. "Fucking hell."

Quinn handed back the keys. "I think we'll walk."

4

BROCK DRAGGED the beast out of the car and dumped it onto the garage floor. While the men lamented the damage to the poor leather seats in the convertible, Erryn eyed the dead body, lying on its back, lacking its head. She swallowed hard. As if sensing her disquiet, Quinn placed a hand on her forearm. A light touch. Reassurance. It felt nicer than she wanted to admit.

And out of place. Dead monster, remember?

She approached it and noted its large size. Close to seven feet, she estimated, given how it towered over the men. Thick, but not overly so. Very muscled. The skin was a mottled gray and brown, matching the fur that coarsely covered its body. It wore no clothes but for a thong. A modest monster? It hid a less-than-modest endowment. From the stump of its neck, blood oozed dark, almost black, and it reeked.

"What stinks?" Brock asked as if reading her mind.

Quinn pointed. "As if you need to ask. Dead body. Probably has gas."

"It's not gas." Her nose wrinkled. "It's more like meat gone bad."

"It just died," Quinn pointed out.

"You think it was a zombie?" Brock exclaimed.

"No. I see no signs of decomposition," she said, pressing her fingers to its flesh and not noticing any squishing. Rigor mortis hadn't yet set in. "Where'd the head go?"

"Rolled to the workbench." Brock pointed to a mass of hair and blood leaning against a metal table strewn with car parts and tools.

She squatted beside it and noted the humanoid features amidst the beastly ones—the eyes wide open and she'd swear fixed in horror. "I'm thinking shapeshifter of some kind. But I couldn't tell you what animal, as it seems like a mishmash of a few." She saw canine—possibly wolf—but there was something else about the beast that struck her. She just couldn't pinpoint what exactly. Was it the way the ears flattened and pointed? The almost leathery texture of its skin in the spots where the fur appeared sparse?

She glanced at the body, the way it lay lopsided on the floor. "Help me flip it over," she asked as she neared it.

Quinn didn't wait but grabbed the body and rolled it chest down, exposing the wings on its back. "Thought I was mistaken earlier. It explains how it got on the roof."

"Doubtful it can fly. These appear stunted," she observed.

"It probably climbed. I've got one of them permanent ladders installed so I can check my equipment," Brock added.

Erryn crouched and ran a hand down a wing and pulled it, murmuring, "These remind me of those of a bat."

"There are no bat shapeshifters," Quinn remarked.

"That we know of," Erryn argued.

"Is this the creature that's been terrorizing the flock?" Quinn directed the question to Brock.

He shrugged. "I think the more important question is, does it have friends?"

Their gazes went to the gaping skylight. Nothing appeared.

Which meant Erryn uttered a sharp cry of alarm when a dulcet voice from behind them said, "It was hunting alone."

Erryn whirled to behold a woman, shapely in form, with a silken hood that covered most of her face. Her eyes were dark pits ringed in midnight lashes that matched the even grimmer outfit she wore—form-molding leather pants, skintight top, soft-soled boots with no heel. Bare handed, but the woman wore a knife sheath on her thigh.

"Lady Arianna, I wasn't expecting you." Brock didn't sound happy.

The lady drawled, "Evidently." She neared and ran a finger over the hood of the blue sports car to the driver's seat. "Did you have to murder it on the leather?"

"The blood will come out," Brock promised.

"But the smell won't, will it, puppy?" Her annoyance showed in her tone and eyes, the only thing revealed of her face.

"I'm so sorry. We should have let the thing maim or kill us to spare the car." Erryn didn't feel one whit bad saying it, although Fred would chastise her if the haughty lady complained about her to the Cabal.

Arianna glanced at Erryn, her eyes drawn in a frown. "No one was talking to you."

"I helped kill it."

"Would you like me to clap?" Arianna chirped. "Now be quiet while I deal with the interloping wolf." Arianna turned her attention to Quinn. "You don't belong here."

"It wasn't my intention to be here. I had a traveling mishap," Quinn explained.

Brock jumped in to add, "This is my friend Quinn. We go way back."

"Since when do you invite your Lycan friends into our territory without permission?" the haughty vampire asked.

Erryn saw Brock clench his fists. The man lived in a delicate balance with the vampires in this country. He couldn't really argue, but Erryn could, so she jumped in. "Don't get pissy at Brock. It wasn't his fault. Like Quinn said, we ran into an issue with our flight, and Quinn thought Brock might be able to help us find an alternative method of travel."

"I am well aware your plane exploded and that people believe you are dead. Unlike those investigating, I am neither stupid nor shortsighted. A Cabal plane can only mean Lycans, and there is only one other puppy in town." Such dripping disdain.

"Aren't you the smart one. You found us," Erryn taunted.

"Indeed, I did, and look at you, not dead." Said so pleasantly. "What's odd about that, though, is it's been hours since the explosion and the Cabal is still convinced you are. I wonder why you wouldn't have contacted them to tell them otherwise."

Erryn snorted. "Please, you and I both know we'd be dumb to call. Someone tried to kill us. Since we can't be sure we don't have a leak inside the Cabal, we need to be cautious."

The fabric of Arianna's silken mask barely puffed as she sighed. "I really don't care if you live or die, but it is my duty to inform you that we don't want any of your doggy fights in our territory. Acts of aggression will be met with force."

"Hold on a second, you can't be blaming us? I will point out that we only stopped here to refuel. Someone in *your* city planted that bomb. Making this a *you* problem," Erryn pointed out.

"It wasn't the flock," hissed Arianna.

"And yet, like you mentioned earlier, this is your territory, and not only did someone attempt to kill two

Cabal members passing through, that thing"—Erryn pointed—"tried to kill us."

"You are most unlikeable," Arianna grumbled.

"But right." And then because her curious mind had to know: "Why are you here in the middle of the night?"

"Vampire. We don't like daylight," Arianna breezily replied.

"Bullshit. You were following the monster," Erryn said almost accusingly.

"Wait, you were following it?" Brock exclaimed. "Alone?"

Arianna growled. "Are you implying something?"

"It's dangerous." Brock dug his misogynistic hole deeper.

Arianna laughed. "Why, puppy, were you actually worried for me? I've wrestled larger."

Brock's expression creased in annoyance. "You shouldn't be so blasé about it. This thing has been killing vamps."

"Who says this beast is responsible?" Arianna countered.

That caused Brock to blow out a breath. "Come on, how many monsters do you think we have running around in the city capable of decapitating vampires with their claws?"

"More than one. I've killed two already, injured a third. Pretty sure there are at least eight out there, maybe more. I haven't been able to track them to their lair. Once they get into the sewers,

51

they disappear." The princess couldn't hide her annoyance.

"You've been tracking them in the sewers?" Erryn hoped Brock didn't explode. He spoke through such a rigid jaw.

"It's where they go after an attack."

"What are they?" Erryn asked.

Arianna shrugged. "I don't know. Many in the flock claim they are mutants. Whatever their origin, they are a menace."

"I've never seen anything like it." Erryn returned to crouch by the head, the nose of it flat and flared, the jaw elongated. The gaping mouth showed teeth, the sharp canines in the front at odds with the human molars behind, one of which held a silver crown reinforcing her belief this was a shifter.

"They began appearing a few months ago and have proven tricky to eliminate." A disgruntled admission from the lady.

"How did you get on the trail of this one?" Quinn asked.

"I wasn't following it but tracking you. As I mentioned earlier, I came here looking for you. This was unexpected." She waved a hand at the dead body. "It makes me wonder why it suddenly changed its modus operandi. Who was it after?"

"I don't think it cared so long as it was trying to kill somebody," Erryn opined.

"Or you were targeted. Where were you flying to?" Arianna's gaze fixed them.

"None of your business."

"I'm making it my business," declared Arianna, her eyes turning dark.

"We're going to Spain," Quinn quickly lied. "Doing Cabal work."

"Since when do your werewolf overlords work with women?" Arianna gazed hard at Erryn as if she could puzzle out her secrets.

"Since I'm useful. We haven't been properly introduced. I'm Doctor Silver." She held out her hand.

A surprised Arianna quickly clasped it, squeezed, and let it go, but not before saying, "I am Lady Arianna. But you may call me milady."

Erryn snorted. "I don't recognize monarchies. They are an archaic system that is disrespectful to the will of the people."

Arianna blinked. "How is it no one has killed you yet?"

"I'm tougher than I look," Erryn replied sweetly.

"You are the doctor who helped deliver the Lycan child in Canada," Arianna suddenly stated.

"You're well informed," Quinn remarked as Brock exclaimed, "Wait, I thought babies were impossible."

Arianna replied before Erryn could. "There are issues with natural-born Lycan. There is an extremely high mortality rate for mothers and children, as they require certain conditions that are hard to meet."

Erryn couldn't help but blurt out, "What do you know about it?" It had never occurred to her to ask the long-lived vampires if they had any knowledge. She'd scoured all the folklore she could gather on the Lycans, spent years going from pack to pack, speaking to elders, seeing what documentation they had. Living out of a motel for most of her life. The irony of studying close-knit packs while she bounced around didn't escape her.

"I know that, despite what the Cabal might have told you, there is no interest in changing their ways. Which explains the plane."

"The Cabal didn't plant the bomb." Erryn wished she could be more certain of that. All signs pointed to a traitor.

"If you say so," the vampire lady sang. "You will be gone by morning." Arianna didn't ask.

"Soon as we can find a way out," Quinn promised.

"And take her with you." Arianna pointed at Erryn.

She almost blew Arianna a kiss but instead tried a more diplomatic. "At a later date, would you be open to discussing what you know of the Lycan?"

The request appeared to surprise the lady. She blinked before saying, "I suppose we can, if you live." Arianna then turned to Brock. "I'll be back next week for my car."

"I'll make sure you never knew a monster died in it."

The lady added a sly, "Can you do anything about the dog smell you always leave behind?"

"Can you do anything about your attitude?" Brock sassed.

Amusement lilted her words. "No. I'll leave you to

say your goodbyes and add a reminder that your friends better leave our territory, or else."

No need to ask what the "else" stood for.

Arianna paused a moment by the side door, entering a code to unlock it. Brock cursed. "She hacked me again."

The mechanism made enough noise Erryn realized Arianna must have entered a different way. But how? She gazed upward. Surely Arianna didn't drop in from above? Vampires didn't fly.

As far as she knew.

Quinn whistled. "She's a prize."

Brock hastened to defend her. "She's not too bad compared to some. She's got to be tough, given she'll be taking over from her dad if he ever croaks."

"Odd how she doesn't know what it is or why it's hunting vampires and now Lycans," Quinn remarked.

"Not our problem," Erryn reminded him.

Quinn grimaced. "I know. But it could be important."

"We have other concerns at the moment, such as getting out of here before her highness returns to make good on her threat."

Brock headed for a board hung with keys. "None of these babies are road ready, but I do have something you can borrow if you don't mind leaving some of your luggage behind."

The reason became clear a moment later as he unveiled the moped under a tarp. It could seat two but forget bringing anything else. Not that it stopped her from slinging her laptop bag across her back.

A smart Quinn didn't say shit about it, even as he dug through his duffel for a jacket. He also handed her a thick sweater that she stuffed under the oversize jacket Brock gave her.

Quinn slung a leg over the saddle seat, assuming he'd drive. She let him have it. She usually stuck to vehicles with four wheels. Once he settled into place, she lifted a leg to climb on behind him, a hand on his shoulder to steady herself. She'd not counted on how she'd feel sitting so close to someone.

Not just anyone. Him.

Only he brought flutters to her tummy and had her breath catching when she slid her arms around his middle, pressing her tight to him. He tensed at first before murmuring, "Whatever you do, don't let go."

"I'm more likely to squeeze you to death," she promised.

To which he chuckled, "Squeeze as hard as you like, Doc."

She really wished he wouldn't tempt her.

5

SILVER WASN'T LYING about hugging Quinn tight. Her arms wrapped around his torso, pressing her against him in an intimate fashion he had a hard time ignoring. With the wind rushing past their faces, her usually unpleasant scent vanished, leaving him...confused.

Usually, he could temper his attraction to her with the wrongness of her aroma. Take that away and he became all too aware of her as a woman.

The late hour meant mostly empty roads, and they made good time to the station. Harder to find a place to park the moped where it wouldn't get stolen. He chose under a bright light in clear view of some CCTV cameras. Given London's vast surveillance network, there was no avoiding his own face or Silver's being captured, although he noted how she kept herself mostly angled so as to prevent a full-face shot.

What did she have to hide?

He had a feeling she knew more than she let on. And he was really beginning to wonder about her involvement with the Cabal. How had she come to their attention? Surely it wasn't just a werewolf attack? An unfortunate amount happened every year, yet she'd been singled out to not only be given access to their secrets but encouraged to dig deeper into them. It made no sense. Surely they had other Lycan doctors they could have turned to.

They left the bike and headed for the terminal, a big building that allowed numerous trains to enter and exit. He had to admire their efficient system when it came to travel.

The departure and arrivals board didn't show much for this time of night. It didn't stop them from buying the first set of tickets available that would take them from England across the channel to Paris.

Within a few hours, they were in the Paris station planning the next leg of their route.

"Finally going to tell me where we're going?" he'd grumbled as she perused the departure board.

"Does it really matter?" she'd asked, not even looking at him

"No, but it would be nice to know."

"If anyone asks, tell them Turkey."

"You think I'd betray you?"

"Not intentionally but there are ways of making people talk."

He glared at her long enough she finally looked him in the face. And sighed.

"Are you going to pout about this?"

"I have a right to know."

She pursed her lips. "Our final destination is Romania."

"Why Romania?"

"You'll see."

He chose not to push her, not in the very public train station at any rate.

It would take more than a day of travel to reach Romania, and given they'd not had a chance to rest, he said nothing when she splurged with the cash she'd brought and reserved them a private cabin. Once inside, they no sooner saw the bunks than they both collapsed, the locked door and moving train doing much to lull them into sleep, where he dreamed.

He'd barely made it to the park, traffic messier than he'd expected. He parked his car and prayed no one would find his hide-a-key as he headed into the woods at a jog.

Quinn could feel it coming, the seventh time since it all happened. The change from man to wolf. He couldn't control it. The moment the moon's rays touched his skin, it would reshape him. He'd tried hiding the last two full moons. Stayed a man. And somehow that was worse. He itched inside his own skin. Restless for...for the wolf.

Hence why tonight he ventured forth, finding a remote park he could shift in.

A bend in the path meant he never saw the other

59

EVE LANGLAIS

couple and almost ran into them. The male snatched his girl off the path and shouted, "Watch out!"

They were the ones that should be careful. Twilight fell, and the full power of the moon would soon strike him. He veered from the set path, not caring if he got lost but knowing he had to get away. Away from the tempting meat, because hunger knotted his stomach.

When he could hold it in no more, it struck him like lightning. He hit his knees on the ground and tore at his clothes, tugging off the shirt first, even as he cursed through a cramping jaw as he pulled at his pants.

And then he had no hands. No words, just yips and grunts. His sense of smell sharpened, and he inhaled deeply, semi orgasming at being so in tune with the world.

If hungry.

He needed to hunt.

The wolf didn't differentiate. Human was as tasty as rabbit. And in this case closer.

He emerged from the woods on silent paws, drooling at the oblivious meat, his prey engaged in an embrace.

These are people. He heard the statement within his mind, both understood it and didn't because they were food.

He snarled in their direction, smelled their fear. Wanted to yell, "run," and barked instead. When the prey jumped and bolted, he started to give chase, only to yelp as something grazed a furrow along his flesh. In his distraction he didn't realize he had company.

Another bullet fired, but this time he was ready and

60

ran. Ran until he found a stream and drank, disgruntled at having lost his supper.

A scent warned him he wasn't alone, and he whirled with a snarl.

I am not alone. Another wolf faced him. His lip peeled back.

Go away.

The other wolf didn't budge. He growled and took a step forward, his gaze locked with the other predator—

Wait. Now it was a man. A very naked man stood in front of him, arms crossed, unabashed.

A werewolf like me.

"Don't be afraid, brother." When the man gestured for him to follow, he trotted close to his heels right into a camp. He roasted his fur by a warm fire as the man spoke. He told him of the Lycan. His history. The rules.

Not all of it stuck given he listened via the consciousness of a newly awakened wolf. But Griffin, the man who found Quinn, taught him what it meant to be Lycan.

The pleasant dream didn't wake him like the nightmares did, and he slept straight for almost eight hours. He woke to find Silver tapping on her computer, smelling awful, as if she'd freshly doused herself in the worst body spray possible. He left to find the washroom on board, cramped but allowing for him to freshen up.

When he returned, it was to find she'd ordered them some food. The tiny table that unfolded gave them a spot to share it and not speak much.

Awkward.

Which was why he decided to dive right into the question nagging him.

"You said the Cabal recruited you after you were attacked. Why?"

"Because I saw a werewolf." She didn't add "duh," but her tone said it all.

"Protocol states that we are supposed to cast doubt on the assertion it's a Lycan attack and shove the narrative that it was a dog."

"Kind of hard to do that when I saw him shift in front of me."

"Which is why those claiming they've seen a werewolf are often accused of being on drugs. But the Cabal didn't discredit or kill you. They hired you."

She leaned back and pursed her lips at him. "Why the interest?"

"Because your involvement with the Cabal doesn't make sense. Unless you're a daughter from before the change."

That caused her to snort. "I have no father. Is it so hard to believe they wanted a woman as a scientist?"

"It's more the fact they went with someone who wasn't a Lycan."

"Perhaps an outsider is more likely to see the things that have been missed."

"There's something you're not telling me," he accused.

"And if there is? What of it? You have your secrets. I have mine. Deal with it," she snapped.

"I have no secrets."

"Oh really? I've seen your file. Griffin didn't make you."

"What are you talking about?" No one knew who bit Quinn. Even Quinn didn't have a name. Griffin had advised him to tell everyone they were old chums from school. No one ever really questioned any further.

"Your Lycan markers don't match."

He blinked.

Erryn smirked. "I am guessing you didn't know that it's possible to identify Lycans with the same change sequence via deep genetic testing."

"I did not."

"It's not information that's been bandied about much given how recently I discovered it."

"Does the biter make a difference?"

"That remains to be seen. Thus far, I've not encountered any differences, but then again, the testing pool has been small and, of course, kept confidential."

"Griffin might not have made me, but he's the one who taught me how to be a Lycan." Told him all the rules. Explained how to handle the hunger. Showed him where to go.

"So who changed you?" she bluntly asked.

"I never knew his name. We were prisoners of war, and those holding us captive knew what he was and forced him to bite us."

"You obviously escaped."

"Yeah, but he didn't survive." Leaving him in those

mountains had been hard, but Scarecrow had insisted. Told them they'd be wasting their strength. After the rescue, he'd gone with a team to find Scarecrow, but the body was gone, taken by scavengers. Kind of like the place where they'd been held prisoner. No one remained alive, and the only evidence of foul play? The blood stains left behind.

"How did you start working for the Cabal?" the doctor asked.

"It just kind of happened. At first, they used to run my jobs through Griffin, asking him if he knew someone to give them a hand. After a few missions, they started contacting me directly."

"Do you like it?" she asked.

He didn't reply right away, mostly because he wasn't sure of a reply. He'd never actually thought of it in terms of like or dislike. After a pause, he said, "I like feeling as if I'm doing something important. I mean don't get me wrong, I enjoy my usual job as security for Griffin's business, but the Cabal missions make me feel alive."

"That I can understand. It's why I jumped on the chance to work for them. Despite my degree, I had little hope of getting my own grant or lab for at least a decade if at all. And then the chance of a lifetime dropped in my lap."

"Only after you were mauled," he pointed out.

She grimaced. "Yeah, that part sucked." The most honest and talkative she'd been since they'd met months ago. He had to wonder at the change.

"What happened? Did the guy lose track of the time and get hit by the moon?"

She drummed her fingers for a second, and he thought she wouldn't reply. When she did, it was low, and he almost missed it. "I don't know. He died that same night."

"Who killed him?"

"My professor."

"Your professor?" His jaw dropped.

"Turns out he was a Lycan too. He saved me."

He blinked. It took him a second to fit the pieces together. "Your professor was part of the Cabal."

She nodded. "Given he knew my abilities, he offered me a job instead of leaving me to die."

"That's very unusual."

"I'm aware." Her reply was flat, unhelpful.

He had more questions, so many, but the train jolted before slowing. The speaker crackled and announced they'd reached a station, the midpoint in their journey, meaning they had to disembark.

The moment for casual chat had passed, and they packed their things in silence. While more curious than ever, he'd have to wait for the next leg of their journey. It would offer plenty of time for the spilling of secrets. Not something he'd expected to do with the brusque Doctor Silver. He actually rather enjoyed her tough streak. As for the times she showed her softer, more vulnerable side? If he wasn't careful, he'd start liking her.

Their next train was delayed, some kind of repair,

which left officials advising travelers to make other arrangements.

Silver wasn't happy about it. "I hate delays."

"We could rent a car."

Her nose wrinkled. "They'll want a credit card, meaning we'll be sending up a giant not-dead flag."

A good point. Stealing a car had the risk of being pulled over. They could ride a bus, or... His gaze went to another train slowly starting to chug past several tracks over. "I've got an idea."

She followed his glance. "That's a cargo train."

"Exactly."

"You want us to hitch a ride?"

"Yup. Come on. Haven't you always wanted to ride the rails?" He winked.

"We don't know where it's going."

"It's going west, which is in the right direction."

She sighed. "You better not put us in a livestock car."

"No promises. Let's go."

The dispersing crowd meant less cover as they slipped off the main platform and crossed tracks. They might have been noticed if not for the scene a woman was making upon hearing her trip would be delayed. While she had a fit, they raced to match speed with the chugging mechanical centipede.

Quinn leaped first, grabbing hold of a bolted bar and finding a spot for his feet. Before he could reach to help Silver, she'd leapt aboard on the car just behind his. She gave him a thumbs-up before disappearing.

The spot he'd chosen had a car with a smooth back, a tanker for fluid. Meanwhile the one she'd leapt across had a door, which opened to show Silver smirking. "Want to come inside?"

He joined her in the mostly empty space. Several straps were strung across and into ringed tethers, crisscrossing over a giant metal bell, the surface of it etched in vines and flowers. There was nothing else in the train car, which meant sitting on the hard, shivering floor. At least they did so side by side because it would be dumb to be at opposite ends.

He grimaced as he said, "Wishing I'd thought to grab some snacks before we hopped the rail."

She smirked. "Good thing I'm the smart one in this duo." She rummaged in her bag and brought out several treats. Chips. Nuts. Even a liter of water.

"Damn, Doc. I'm impressed."

"I like to be prepared. You never know what will happen."

"You always expect the unexpected?"

She shrugged. "Life isn't always easy. I like to be prepared. And before your nosy ass asks, this doesn't come from some past trauma. I was raised by my mom, had a very normal childhood. I went to school. Got great grades."

"You close to your mom?"

She shook her head. "She passed when I was in university. What about you?"

He grimaced. "Inner-city kid with six older brothers. Mom died when I was young, and so I got shuffled around between my aunts and uncles, who barely had enough for themselves let alone another kid. Soon as I turned eighteen, I enlisted and got away."

"Did you have any kids before you were turned?"

"Nope." He shook his head. "And I was warned by the guy who bit me to not get anyone pregnant. I got the big snip soon as I could."

"Do you regret it?" she asked.

"Honestly? Was never really into the whole kid thing. I mean that baby Ulric had is cute and all, but..." He shrugged. "I'm not cut out to be a dad. What about you?"

She snorted. "Do I seem the maternal type?"

He grinned. "Well, you are awfully interested in Lycan babies."

"I'm interested in them for medical reasons."

Because she seemed open to talk, he broached it. "What did you really give Honey to make sure she wouldn't lose the kid?"

"Vitamin shots."

He made a noise. "Come on. I'm not stupid. That was more than vitamins."

She pursed her lips before saying, "Because of my research, I might have added a little something to her doses."

"That's why she and the baby survived."

"Most likely." She sighed. "But you can't tell anyone."

"Isn't that like good news, though?"

"Depends how you look at it. What if Lycans could have babies without fear?"

"That would be amazing."

"What if those babies can shift?"

He blinked. "I thought baby Michael was human."

"He is. For now. But he has the marker."

"Meaning what?"

"Meaning he could shift. Maybe the next moon. Maybe never. Or maybe it will happen when he least expects it. Do you know how many supposed dog attacks happen every year in the city? And how many of those supposed dogs are never found? Why just a few months ago, there was a wolf shot in downtown New York of all places. Witnesses claimed he came out of nowhere in the crowd at some concert in the park."

"Maybe he got bitten but never got told what it meant." Quinn might have made that same mistake if he'd not had some warning.

"I think that, despite the laws and precautions, some Lycans have tried to have babies. And I further believe some have succeeded."

"If you figured out the secret vitamin, maybe they did too."

"Ah yes, because so many pregnant women are willing to take wolfsbane."

"You're kidding. Wolfsbane? Isn't that like poisonous?"

"To humans, yes."

"Honey is human," he reminded.

"But her child isn't," Erryn pointed out. "A small

dosage of it didn't appear to harm her, and it inhibited the child's Lycan side, allowing her to carry it to term."

His mouth rounded. "Holy shit. You put its wolf to sleep during the pregnancy." A simple way of putting it. He then slapped his leg. "If it's that easy, why the fuck are we still making guys get vasectomies?"

"There are a few reasons. One being that wolfsbane doesn't always work to suppress the change, and it loses effectiveness on a full moon. You saw how Honey reacted when exposed."

"The baby wanted to shift." He frowned. "The only problem with that theory is Michael's almost three months now. He's seen two full moons and not turned into a puppy yet."

"I have a theory about that. I think in the womb, the excess hormones passed on from the mother do something to boost the shifting ability. Once the child is born, those levels return to normal."

"Wouldn't that mean they'd start shifting as soon as they hit their teens?"

"I don't know because I've never been able to study one."

"If they even exist. Surely we'd have found some by now."

"How?" she asked with an arch of her brow. "It's not as if someone shifting alone would know to contact the Cabal or seek out a pack. They'd assume they were unique. Alone."

"You're assuming a Lycan had a child with a

human and then never bothered to tell them anything of their heritage."

"What if they didn't think they had to? Maybe they assumed the child couldn't shift without a bite?" she countered. "Would they have risked their secret in that case?"

"You make it sound impossible to find someone who might have been born from a Lycan father."

"Almost. Unless you're looking for the right signs."

"And you saw them in this place we're going to in Romania?"

"I did." She paused and then explained. "I've uncovered five hits from a DNA ancestry place that indicate there are individuals with the Lycan gene in a small town called Gherdeal."

"Could be someone formed an illegal pack."

"Guess we'll soon find out."

"Soon?" He laughed. "I wish. We've got hours to go, Doc. Long enough for you to tell me more about you."

"This isn't a date," she tersely replied.

"You got something better to do?"

"We should be resting."

"I'm not tired," he stated.

"I am," she totally lied.

He wondered why. Why was she so open one minute and shut down the next?

And most of all, why the fuck did it bother him?

6

SHUT *it down before I say something dumb.*

Erryn couldn't have said what prompted her to be so frank with Quinn. Could it be she tired of keeping secrets? Or did Quinn have something about him that just made her trust him? Whatever the reason, she'd told him more than she'd told anyone but her mentor.

Which was to say too much. But at least he didn't know her biggest secret.

She pretended to be tired and stripped Brock's coat and lay it on the floor to give her a layer from the radiating chill. She lay down and pillowed her head on her lumpy bag.

Quinn didn't stop her—or join her, for that matter —but remained sitting. Pity. She could have used the warmth of his body, given the sweater she wore didn't do much to fight the chill invading the car.

She must have shuddered a little too much because suddenly the heavy weight of his coat covered her. She sat upright. "I don't need it," she protested, trying to hand it back.

"You're freezing."

"I'll live."

"So will I," he said sarcastically. "Probably better than you. Instead of arguing, take it and get some rest."

"You should sleep too," she noted.

"Someone should keep watch."

"From what?" she asked. "Do you seriously expect anyone to come roaming through here while we're in motion?"

"No. But we should be careful."

"No one is going to find us," she stated, and he clucked his tongue.

"Now you've gone and done it. Tempted the fates."

"Don't tell me you're superstitious?"

"Aren't you?"

"I'm a doctor."

"A doctor who knows that Lycans are not creatures defined by conventional medicine or science."

"The change is biological."

"With a hint of what the fuck," he added.

No denying that. "Everything has an answer. Sometimes it just takes longer to find. A few hundred years ago we blamed witches for every piece of bad luck."

"You will do anything not to admit magic and mysticism are real."

"Are you a man who can't handle a woman having her own opinion?" was her tart reply.

He arched a brow. "Is that how we're going to play? Gotcha. Guess we'll see shortly if karma is gonna slap you for what you said."

"Don't be so paranoid. We'll be fine."

"If you say so." He slid down, arms crossed on his chest, barely visible in the faint outside light coming in through the windows in the doors on either end.

Seeing him willing to freeze had her blurting out, "We should share body heat."

She felt more than saw him stiffen but most definitely saw white teeth gleaming as he grinned. "I'm in. Who gets to be the little spoon?"

"Me, because I'd barely cover half of you."

"Okay, but I warn you, I am merely a man, and you might not know this, but used to be if the wind blew in just the right way, I'd get a hard-on. Then again, as a doctor, you'd know that the body is conditioned to react under certain types of stimuli."

"Would you control it better if I told you I have no interest in you?" Erryn lied, glad he couldn't really see her face in the dark.

"Neither do I, but for some reason, I'm still attracted to you."

"That makes no sense."

"I know," he grumbled.

"How about I ignore your teenage boner and we get some sleep? Think you can manage not to give in to your lust?"

"I wouldn't force anyone," he huffed.

"I know. Jeezus. Why am I arguing?" she

exclaimed. "You don't want to be warm, then freeze." With that, she flung herself onto her side, facing away from him.

"Are you always this dramatic?" he drawled, even as he rolled and slid closer. The coat draping her lifted as he drew near, his body curving around hers.

Arousal hit her, pulsing between her legs. Apparently, he wasn't the only one who couldn't control himself. Here was to hoping he didn't smell it.

Thinking of smell had her cringing. She'd not bathed since Brock's place and, while less than a day, felt the grime of travel on her.

A hand hit her waist and rested there as he huffed hotly, her hair not enough to hide the whisper of his words, "Is my hand okay?"

She almost said no because she wanted it somewhere else. She mumbled, "It's fine."

"Mind if I position my other arm here?" He slid it under her neck and head, the bicep wide enough to pillow.

It was nice. "Comfortable now?" she queried instead.

His hand slid to cup her belly.

Instant quiver between her thighs.

"Now, I'm good," he murmured.

"You sure? Or do you need to grope me some more?" she said sarcastically while, at the same time, part of her hoped he would. She couldn't remember the last time she wanted someone to touch her so badly.

"Is that an invitation?" He spoke close to her ear, and she shivered.

She wanted to turn in his arms and see what would happen. It had been so long since her last disastrous attempt.

The fingers on his hand spread, covering a good portion of her. His body followed the line of hers, the warmth of him more than expected. Soothing. Exciting.

Dangerous.

She knew better than to have sex.

Ever.

It never ended well. Look what happened to Joseph.

Focusing on the fallout if she gave in to fleeting desire helped her fight it. And Quinn didn't push it.

It led to her falling asleep and dreaming of that fateful night.

They entered the lab after hours, Joseph having a key from the professor, given he'd volunteered to set up things for their class the next day.

But they weren't there to get a head start on their next lesson.

Joseph grabbed her around the waist and dragged her close. They'd been dating for the last three weeks. Sleeping together finally in the past few days. Finding privacy when they both had roommates made it challenging. Then again, having sex in cramped, windowless closets and bathroom stalls did up the excitement factor.

Joseph had brought a blanket and spread it on a stainless-steel counter by the window. How romantic, especially since the clouds had shifted to let the full moon shine.

She went to kiss Joseph, only to find him grimacing. "What's wrong?"

"I don't feel right." He leaned back against the counter and rubbed his face, the back of his hands hairier than she recalled.

"Joseph?" She queried his name as he began to shake. Only he turned from her, gripping the blanket he'd just spread and making grunting noises. It was the rippling of his body that had her taking a step back, though.

He appeared to be having a seizure the likes of which she'd never heard of despite all the medical books she'd studied.

His body humped and hitched. His clothing tore as he hit the floor on his knees and hands. Fur sprouted from flesh. Legs turned to hairy limbs ending in paws. A head lifted, the smooth cheeks pushed out into a muzzle.

Joseph was gone and in his place a wolf.

A wolf who turned its gaze on her and growled.

Oh shit.

Before she could run, Joseph lunged, and she barely had time to lift an arm. Sharp teeth clamped onto her flesh. Biting. Piercing her skin. The pain excruciating. She couldn't help but scream. And scream.

"Shhh."

A voice shushed and roused her from the night-

77

mare she'd not had in years. She found herself still cradled against Quinn, his body tense.

"I'm sorry," she whispered, assuming fault.

"Don't be. Nightmares suck."

They did. Especially since she knew she was to blame for Joseph dying that night.

Quinn's hand on her belly rubbed lightly in soothing circles. She wanted it lower. Maybe things would be different with him. She'd never been with a Lycan. Never dared.

What if he said no?

The erection against her said otherwise.

She grabbed hold of his hand and slid it down to the apex of her thighs. Madness and yet she moaned the moment he cupped her. He didn't say anything as he stroked her through her pants, titillating her enough her hips arched and breathing quickened. He slid a hand into the front of her trousers, the comfortable material stretching to accommodate. He found her moist slit and dampened a finger before circling it over her clit.

She should stop this. This really wasn't the time or place.

His lips touched her earlobe and tugged.

She gasped, and her hips jerked.

He fingered her, the heel of his hand rubbing her clit. He sucked on her ear, the hotness of his breath teasing.

Her breath caught as a mini orgasm took her.

Too quick.

Not enough. She turned to face him, the darkness hiding his expression, making this safe for her. His mouth was ready for hers when they touched.

Their breaths mingled, as did their tongues and lips. Her throbbing pussy welcomed the hard press of his thigh. She rode it and panted as they kissed. She was reaching for his pants when he suddenly murmured against her mouth, "We have company."

It took her a second to process. "I didn't hear the door open."

"Outside. I can hear vehicles, and the train is slowing down." Even as he said it, there was a loud blart of the horn. A warning.

She sat upright, desire forgotten as preservation kicked in. "You think we've been found?"

He rose to his feet and shrugged. "Could be a random border inspection."

"But?" she pressed.

"Never hurts to be cautious."

The train screed as the brakes were applied. The rough stoppage had Quinn throwing out a hand to grip the wall of the car and the other steadying her, even though she didn't need it.

"The train isn't moving." A dumb and obvious thing to say. "Should we stay in the car or get out now?"

"I think we should figure out what's going on first."

"If it's border guards, we'll be arrested."

"If they find us. Could be a robbery, in which case I doubt they'll be interested in the bell."

"A land heist? I thought most criminals preferred pirating?" Easier to get away at sea.

"Thieves don't care when or how they steal." He ducked in for a hard kiss and a whispered, "Stay here while I check things out."

"I'm not hiding like a coward," Erryn hotly retorted.

"It's called prudence. Not to mention, guarding you is my job. So sit your cute little ass down and let me do it."

She eyed him and pressed her lips into a line. "So much misogyny in that one sentence."

"Calling your ass little and cute isn't sexist but the truth. Do you have any idea how pissed I am someone chose now to interrupt our trip? My balls hurt so bad I might just die."

She blinked. Surely he jested. Erryn didn't inspire that level of passion. "If you're that sensitive, you should see a doctor."

"A doctor is my entire problem," he growled. "Never had an issue before. And now? Now I'm a fucking idiot who needs to hit something. Stay here," he barked before he exited.

She thought about following him because, hello, he did not give her orders. But at the same time, given the situation, she should be cautious. In that spirit, she exited via the opposite door. After all, two eyes were better than one, and he seemed to forget she'd saved his butt in the last fight.

Emerging from the car, she noted night still

reigned. The sky remained dark, barely a moon tonight given the wispy clouds. But more terrifying? The train was stopped on a bridge, and she could hear the distant rumble of vehicles and voices shouting.

This wasn't a border check.

Quickly, she grabbed the handholds she could find and clambered to the top of the car, wanting a better view. She didn't count on being dizzied at the sight of the gorge below them. *Don't fall*.

She kept low to ensure she didn't lose her balance. Her new position on the roof allowed her to get a sense of the situation. They, indeed, had company.

A pickup truck appeared to be sitting across the tracks ahead of them, visible because of a slight curve right after the bridge. The parked truck had a light bar illuminating the front of the train. A glance behind showed a second vehicle blocked the rear, only its lights visible.

A crew member emerged from one of the four locomotives powering the train, waving his arms, most likely questioning the halting of their trip. His yelling abruptly ceased, as those who'd spilled from the trucks aimed a gun at him. Some of the hijackers went inside the idling locomotives, and soon the remaining conductors were ejected and tossed to the ground.

A robbery in progress. Only they didn't appear to be taking anything from the cargo cars. A few of the crew got slapped. One of those crumpled on the ground shrieked as someone grabbed them by the hair and hauled them to their feet.

Are they going to kill them? She hoped not. She couldn't stand by and do nothing if that happened.

The thugs doing the abusing continued to yell. While two remained with guns trained on the crew, the others suddenly began walking back, leaving the locomotive section, heading for the cargo. By the second box, it became clear they were looking for something.

Or someone.

Erryn flattened herself fast and hard, lest they look up and spot her. Since she couldn't see as well while pancaked, she inched forward, wondering where Quinn was.

Someone yelled from the rear of the train. She slid around on her belly, saw nothing but she did hear the sharp crack of a gun.

The hollering intensified, as did the popping of weapons. Then silence, from behind at least. In the front? Those searching had gone quiet and hid.

It had to be Quinn. He must have taken out some of the hijackers. And here she lay, a damsel in waiting.

It would have helped if she had a gun, but all she had were her wits and the element of surprise. She rose and ran lightly from the roof of her car to the next, moving to the front. Toward danger.

Call it instinct because it certainly defied logic, but she had a feeling she needed to get off the bridge.

What of Quinn? Could she warn him without giving her position away?

"She's on the roof!"

No mistaking which *she* they spoke of. She put on some speed and ran, yelling since she'd lost her element of surprise. "Quinn."

Hopefully he would follow her off the bridge because her sense of impending doom increased. She was only two cars away from the passenger one and engine.

That was when the man appeared ahead of her, a big and burly fellow that would be difficult to knock down. Of more concern, the gun in his hand. He aimed it at her but never had a chance to fire. The bullet hole in his forehead made sure of that.

The would-be murdering thug toppled, and she whirled to see Quinn. His eyes glowed, body bristling with adrenaline.

"I told you to hide," he growled, voice more beast than man.

"We have to get off this bridge!" she stated.

Before they could move, an explosion shook everything, sending her to her knees.

When the shuddering stilled, she had barely pushed to her feet when an arm swept her up and began moving.

"Run!"

It didn't matter how fast they moved. They were on the roof of the passenger train when the bridge groaned and twisted. The moment the track fell, the car began sliding with it.

And gravity came for Erryn's ass.

7

THE TRAIN CAR tilted in the direction of the collapsing track. They had to get off. Now!

Quinn tightened his grip on Erryn and pushed with his legs, propelling them into the air. They leaped, but not as far as he'd hoped. They slammed into the side of the mountain and started to slide down. His free hand clawed, looking to find anything to stop their plummet. A snapped and dangling support cable proved to be the lifeline he needed. His fingers curled around it and halted their descent with a jolt that had Erryn hooking her leg around him along with her arms.

He still held her tight with his other arm, but he'd need to let go to climb.

As if reading his mind, she reached for the cable and grabbed it above his hand, taking her weight off him. Hand over hand, she strained and pulled herself up, showing a wiry strength he'd not expected. How many more surprises did the doc have in store?

And why did he want to ferret them out?

Not the time to worry about it. He planted his feet and wrapped the cable around his arm, watching the doc to make sure she didn't falter. Ready to catch her if she did.

She paused before the top, a foot braced in shattered concrete, peeking over the edge.

From here, even with the whistle of wind in the canyon, he could hear sobbing and shouting. One woman began to scream, shrilly. A fleshy smack followed, and the crying cut off abruptly.

The doc suddenly ducked and hissed, "Someone's coming to check. Hide."

Easier said than done. The locomotive engine teetered on the edge, making it the only thing that could conceal them.

"Follow," he whisper-shouted as he walked sideways, his grip on the cable the only thing stopping him from a plummet to the death.

She held tight and slid over with him, only to release the cable, given she had less slack to work with. He felt a moment of anxiety as she wedged her feet and hands to slide into a spot between the cracked rail and the cliff. Just in time. They'd no sooner hidden under the precariously perched train than someone appeared at the edge, illuminated by the still glaring truck lights.

The hijacker spent a moment looking down then frowned in their direction, most likely because the shadows made it impossible to see. The guy squinted and crept closer, even reaching to put a hand on the train when it gave a metallic groan.

The guy jumped and moved away. Good, because Quinn had to climb high enough on the cable he could lean against Erryn's legs. They both hugged the wall as the train seesawed into the void. The jagged and bent track angling off the edge saved them from plummeting with it.

"They're leaving," Erryn murmured within seconds of them narrowly missing death, having once more lifted high enough to peek on the situation. Before he could tell her to wait, she'd heaved herself over the edge.

He quickly followed, pushing to his feet and, in that same instance, capturing the chaos. The ambushed passengers milled around in confusion and noise. Those responsible were getting back in the truck, readying to leave. They thought Quinn and Erryn dead.

Fuckers tried to kill them.

Again.

Whether the same group as the plane or not didn't matter. It was starting to piss Quinn off. He stalked toward them, uncaring that the train crew saw him and exclaimed. The guys in the truck were backslapping and laughing, already forgetting what they'd done. As if their deaths didn't matter. Even worse, they'd most likely come after him and the doc again.

Quinn hated loose ends.

He ran for the truck. The bright light bar was easy

to avoid and created a better camouflage than night alone, as it blinded the thugs riding in the vehicle. As the wheels humped over the tracks slowly, readying to turn around, Quinn caught up to it. He'd lost the gun he'd stolen when he handled the guys in charge of the ambush at the rear of the train, but he had other ways to harm.

He leaped and grabbed hold of the lip of the truck's bed, vaulting inside, startling the thugs who thought they were making a clean getaway. Before they could react, Quinn tossed one over the side while seizing his gun in the same motion. He then swung it like a bat, knocking out another before aiming it at the rear window. He didn't fire, though, as the truck emptied. The king-sized cab spilled four more people, all of them with guns in various stages of motion.

Fuck. At least he had the advantage of height. He picked off two before his weapon jammed. A third thug managed to score a line across his arm. He dove at the fucker before he could fire again, driving him into the ground. The fellow didn't give up and tried to jam his thumbs into Quinn's eyes. He head-butted the guy hard enough to stun him, and then he slammed the fucker's skull on the ground until he stopped moving.

He'd learned his lesson in the war. Leaving them alive meant they could sneak up, kill your buddy, and capture your ass.

Never again.

As he pushed to his knees, he heard the scuff of a

step. His head swiveled to the bumper of the truck in time to see a muzzle aimed at his face.

Bang.

Quinn blinked and not because he'd been shot.

The guy fell over, leaving Erryn standing behind, holding a gun. Her expression was flat but her eyes fierce.

"Thanks, Doc. Guess you *are* good at saving lives," he said with a wink.

She blew out a breath. "Let's get out of here before someone starts taking pictures."

They got into the truck, her on the driver's side. Tires crunched the gravel on the sides of the track, spitting it at the train crew, who belatedly ran in their wake, hoping for a ride. They didn't stop. Someone would be along soon to rescue them.

The truck bounced and flew along the tracks until she found a road, and then she immediately veered and drove fast, taking turns that somehow kept them heading southwest.

"Do you know where you're going?" he eventually asked. The truck didn't have a GPS navigation screen, just a radio that played CDs.

"Not really, but I figure we'll eventually see a sign and follow it."

"What do we have to our name?" he asked. She'd lost her laptop bag.

"I've got some cash strapped to me, along with my satellite phone and passport. You?"

"Just my wallet. Phone was in my jacket. Give me yours." He held out his hand.

"It's in one of my pockets. Can't it wait?"

"No. I'll hold the wheel while you find it."

She grumbled under her breath as he kept them on road, and she dug into an inner pocket and held out her phone. "Here."

"Thanks." He opened the window of the truck and tossed it out.

"What are you doing?"

"We're being tracked."

"Not with my phone we aren't," she insisted.

"Can you one hundred percent guarantee that?"

Her lips pursed. "No. Maybe it was a coincidence. We're assuming it was us they were looking for."

"Seems kind of far-fetched to think they weren't," he drawled. "Come on, Doc. You're smart. Someone obviously does not want us to dig into this whole natural-born Lycan thing. And by someone, I mean the Cabal."

"Disrespecting the people you work for?" Her tone was caustic.

"More like being realistic."

"Your logic doesn't work, though, because they sent me on this mission."

"You're assuming they all agreed. Could be there's dissent in their midst. Or someone fears losing their grip on power."

"They do not like change," she muttered.

"Still don't see why you care so much about this,"

he replied as they went by a sign in a language he couldn't understand.

"I don't like secrets."

"Says the lady with a few." A guess but he knew he'd gotten it right when her lips pinched.

"As if I'd share everything with a veritable stranger."

"I'm hurt, Doc. We've known each other for months."

"A few sentences exchanged here and there isn't much."

"That's the old us, Doc. In the past few days, I'd say we've finally made it to the conversation stage of our friendship."

"We're not friends." A hasty counterclaim.

"Odd thing to say given we almost became lovers back on that train."

No denying the heat in her cheeks and the scent of her arousal. It hardened him instantly as if he had no control. Blame the fact that obnoxious scent she liked to wear had worn off. It meant finally getting a real taste of her. Why did she hide her natural sweetness? He couldn't get enough of it. It had him craving her in a way he'd never imagined but had often mocked.

Was this what happened to his friends? They met a woman whose smell drove them a little crazy and led to them saying and doing things they usually avoided?

He'd spooned and fingered his mission. And he'd bloody well do it again, if only to quench the need burning inside.

However, she didn't seem inclined to remember or repeat that crazy, passionate moment. When they finally found a hostel to stay in a few miles out of town —which they walked to, having ditched the traceable truck in a lake—he insisted on two single beds. She reverted back to the cold doctor with the foul scent. The bus they hopped to finish their trip proved silent because they were in different rows.

He couldn't help watching her.

Wondering why she pretended nothing had happened between them.

Wondering why he cared.

The bus dumped them a distance from their destination, meaning they had to bribe a ride to the tiny little town of Gherdeal, which the internet claimed was pretty much abandoned. A place of stone buildings and thatched roofs. Chimneys billowed smoke, as they burned wood and coal for warmth. Electrical poles marred the old-town vibe with their ugly strung wires.

Their steps clonked on cobblestones as they walked the main street with its two shops and three restaurants. The moment they entered the restaurant that looked busiest, all heads turned to look. Stare.

And sniff.

Fuck.

Quinn froze in place as three of the largest males in the place rose to face them. He didn't need to see the gleam in their gazes to know they were Lycan. He'd wager pretty much every guy in the place was.

Silver noticed it as well and muttered, "I think we found the place."

"No shit, Doc." The question being, could they escape?

The jangle of the bell at his back indicated his exit had been blocked.

The situation seemed rather dire until he heard a familiar voice. "What the fuck are you doing here?"

He turned and took in the sight of Gunner before drawling, "I could ask the same. Since when do you wear plaid?"

8

ERRYN KEPT a wary gaze on the restaurant's patrons even after they sat at a sturdy wooden table with Quinn's friend. Another military buddy, although this one appeared to be an unexpected coincidence.

"What are you doing here?" Quinn asked, choosing the outside seat beside Erryn across from his friend.

She didn't like being trapped in a corner, especially since she couldn't help but rub up against the man currently annoying her.

"Looking for answers. I'm surprised to see you here, though," Gunner said.

"We're also looking to solve some questions." Quinn kept it vague.

Gunner's gaze flitted to Erryn then back to Quinn. "You haven't introduced your friend."

To her surprise, Quinn growled. "She's more than a friend." His arm went around her smoothly. She didn't slap it off, curious as to why he laid claim. Because she had no doubt that he was essentially marking her with his words and actions.

Gunner arched a brow. "Congratulations?" The sarcasm only deepened Quinn's scowl.

No wonder the guy didn't believe him.

She tucked into the crook of Quinn's shoulder, trying to play the part of more-than-a-friend. Whatever that meant. "I'm Erryn." She held out her hand.

Gunner stared at it.

"That's Gunner," Quinn jumped in to say. "We used to serve together. He escaped with me and Brock."

She withdrew her hand. "Were you bitten by the same Lycan?"

It seemed impossible, yet Gunner's eyed widened. "What have you told her?"

Quinn softly said, "I don't have to tell her anything since she already knows more than most. She works for the Cabal."

"And so do you," Gunner said almost accusingly as he leaned back with a sneer. "I am surprised you still haven't caught on to their tricks. The Cabal have it good. Accountable to no one and yet sticking their nose in everything."

"They're just trying to keep our kind safe," Quinn argued.

Gunner didn't back down. "Our kind are only one video away from being exposed. We can't keep hiding."

"Says the guy living in a small town in Romania."

"Says the guy in the only town where Lycans can live openly with humans without fear," Gunner uttered with pride.

The news shocked. Erryn blinked. "Everyone here knows?"

"Yes. We're up to over a hundred citizens."

The number floored her. "The Cabal doesn't show a registered Pack for this area," she stated.

Gunner's lips curled. "Because we're a community, not a pack where a rotten alpha calls the shots. We elect those in charge. We vote on our laws."

"And how does someone join?" Erryn asked, wondering how to ask if the Lycans in this town were made or born.

"Initially, it was actually one single extended family where the males became Lycan after they're sired a few children. Over time, even the husbands of the daughters were changed. The town grew, but slowly. Not everyone took to the change, but all agreed to keep the secret. In time, word got around, and loners, like me, happened by and were allowed to settle."

"They take any Lycans?" Quinn sounded shocked by the idea.

"So long as they follow the rules."

"When you say rules, what does that mean?" Quinn queried.

"Thou shalt not shift in front of tourists nor piss to mark your neighbor's property. No killing of wildlife in town. Hunt only in the woods."

Sounded rather reasonable.

"What of those who break the rules?" Erryn asked.

"There are ways of dealing with them."

She wanted to know more, but Quinn leaned forward. "How have you been? Last time I saw you, you were looking kind of rough."

Gunner shrugged. "Was feeling rough. You and Brock took the whole Lycan thing better than me. My journey to acceptance wasn't as smooth."

"And now?" Quinn prodded.

"I've made peace with my fate and chosen to embrace it."

"I'm glad, brother."

"Given your surprise at seeing me, I'm wondering why you're here. The Cabal doesn't have jurisdiction in this town."

"We're not looking to cause trouble," Quinn soothed. "Just seeking some information."

"What kind?" Gunner remained tight-lipped.

Erryn dove right in. "Have the Lycans in town been making babies?"

The blunt question had Gunner blinking at her. "Excuse me?"

"It's a simple question."

Gunner swept a hand. "It's a stupid one. Everyone knows Lycans are made."

"You're sure of that?"

Once more, he stared at her before growling, "What kind of bullshit is this? We can't have babies.

The whole werewolf thing makes pregnancy fatal to women."

"So all the Lycans in town are fixed?"

"Why the fuck are you even asking?"

"She's a doctor," Quinn stated as if that explained it all.

"I've been studying Lycanthropy for the last decade. More recently, whether or not children can be born safely."

"Not. And before you ask, it's been tried."

She leaned forward. "And?"

"And the mothers died. Horribly, I should add." Gunner's lips flattened. "The most recent case was a young girl and her boyfriend. It was thought the bite didn't work since he didn't change during the full moon. He changed the next one, and his girlfriend, who was barely a month pregnant..." He hung his head.

The sorrow hit her. There had to be a way to avert this kind of tragedy. She'd helped one pregnant woman to the finish line, but could she do it again?

"Are there notes or case files from those pregnancies I could read?"

Gunner leaned back. "I don't see why the interest."

"Call it scientific curiosity."

"And it led you here?" Gunner couldn't contain an incredulous note.

"Some of your younger residents have done those trendy DNA tests that exhibited the Lycanthropy marker. Given we showed no active packs in the area, the Cabal granted me permission to look into it."

He waved a hand. "The Cabal is obviously fucking with you because they've known about this place for at least the last ten years."

Her lips pursed. "According to you."

"Don't believe me? Ask them." Gunner smirked.

"I will." Even as she knew the answer. Most likely the Cabal had tried to bury knowledge of this place because it presented an alternative to their rule.

"Where are you staying?" Gunner asked as food arrived without request, a steaming bowl of chunky stew with a crusty warm bread. They must have looked hungry.

Erryn dug in with relish as Quinn handled his friend's query. "Not sure yet. Any suggestions? Also, we need to get some clothes and toiletries. We were robbed while travelling."

"I'm sure I can wrangle you something. And you're in luck. I know a woman who rents out her attic. It's not fancy, but it's got a bed big enough for two and its own bathroom. Includes breakfast, too, if you're up early enough."

While she kept eating, Quinn replied, "Sounds good. We could both use a shower and sleep."

But first, food. She emptied her bowl and sopped the last drop with bread before Gunner led them back outside. Twilight was just starting, their trek only a few minutes to reach a quaint cottage of weathered stone with a peaked roof. The old woman who answered chattered at Gunner in Romanian. Erryn couldn't understand a word, but Gunner, with stilted speech and hand gestures, soon had the old lady grinning.

He turned to them. "So Velma is delighted to rent you the room upstairs. Breakfast is at dawn. Dinner is extra. And no sex, as she doesn't want to listen to it."

Erryn barely held on to her composure.

Quinn drawled, "It's only for a night or two. I'm sure we'll survive."

She couldn't have said what possessed her to tuck tight to him and glance up fake lovingly to purr, "It won't be easy."

His eyes widened slightly, and his lips twitched.

Gunner cleared his throat. "A friendly warning. I wouldn't recommend wandering around at night."

"I thought humans and Lycan existed in harmony," was Erryn's tart reply to the restriction.

"They do, but they don't like strangers. Especially nosy Cabal ones."

"Good to know," Quinn quipped.

Gunner left, the door closing behind him, and Quinn muttered, "He's hiding something."

Obviously. And so were the Cabal if they knew about this place. If only she had a phone, she could have called Fred and asked him what the hell. When she'd planned her trip, he'd not once hinted at what she'd find. Intentional lie or ignorance?

Their hostess chattered at them, and Quinn shook his head. "I'm sorry. I don't understand."

Velma lifted her hand and offered a heavily accented, "Vait."

They waited as she scurried into a room and emerged with some clothes. Simple, soft, pre-worn but it didn't matter. They had nothing else. Erryn accepted her small pile with a smile.

"Thank you."

Velma nodded and smiled. Waved and then disappeared into the back of the house. Erryn eyed the stairs, which were more like a ladder given their open treads and steep incline.

"You want me to go first?" he asked.

"No." She doubted anyone hid up there.

She held the rungs as she climbed into a larger space than expected. One room with built-ins under the slanted sections. The large bed sat on a brass frame, tarnished in some spots, covered in a patchwork quilt with two pillows. The bathroom was literally a toilet and sink hidden by a curtain. The tub? Sat under the only window, which let in waning afternoon light. A small table with mismatched chairs and a dresser completed the space.

"This is nice," Erryn said.

"Sure beats a hotel room." He dumped his armful of clothes on the bed. She placed hers more carefully beside it, doing her best to not look—and imagine—what would happen in the bed they'd share.

A repeat of their earlier petting session with a more climatic ending?

"Who gets first dibs at the bath?" She jerked a

thumb at it, already craving the hot water that would sluice the road from her skin.

"You go ahead. I want to see what Gunner's up to. Maybe check out the town."

"Disobeying him on the first night?" she teased.

"Something's not right."

"In what sense?" she asked.

"Call it a gut feeling."

The last time his gut spoke they'd escaped an exploding aircraft.

"Be careful," was all she said.

Quinn headed for the little sink and ran the tap, leaning down to sluice his face. He lifted a wet face that he patted dry with a towel, saying, "I'm surprised your buddies at the Cabal didn't warn you ahead of time that this place showed a heavy prevalence of Lycan because it was an unregistered pack. They could have stopped you from wasting your time."

"If your friend told the truth."

"Why would he lie?" he countered.

"Or maybe he's not, and only a select few in the Cabal are aware of this autonomous zone."

"Why would they hide it from the others?"

"A good question. The Cabal isn't known for being understanding about those who break their rules, so they must have a reason for allowing it to exist outside their edicts."

"Are they allowing it? Or is it because they know they can't actually do anything about it? You've seen how big this place is."

She shook her head. "Size wouldn't matter. If they've known about this place a decade, then why not squash it when it was small enough to handle? They didn't, meaning the Cabal most likely wanted to see what would happen if Lycans were left to rule themselves."

"And?" Quinn queried.

"And from the sounds of it, they've adopted many of the same rules."

"I hear a but."

"I said many rules, not all. Such as the one about pregnancy."

"You heard Gunner. He said it only happens by accident because of the whole mortality issue."

"Do you really think he'd admit it?" she scoffed. "Not to mention, I already know it's happening. Some of those DNA results I was talking about? They were in people under the age of twenty."

"Maybe they were changed early," he argued weakly.

"Two of them were female."

He blinked. "What?"

"You heard me."

"Women can't be Lycan."

"Women can't be bitten to become Lycan," she corrected. "But what if they were born?"

"Why is it you're only telling me this now?" An angry huffed question.

"Because you didn't need to know."

"I thought we were partners on this trip," he ground out through a tight jaw. "You don't trust me."

"I don't trust anyone." The sad truth.

"Hope one day you can." He didn't offer himself.

As if she needed him or anyone. She sauntered to the tub. She really wanted to soak. But with him in the room, it would be...much too titillating. The man took up all the space. In the room. In her mind.

"When are you leaving?"

"In a few hours. I want the town to settle down for the night before I go wandering."

"Oh." She couldn't help the slump of her shoulders.

"I was kidding before. If you want a bath now, I'll turn my back to give you privacy. I'm not a perv."

She almost said, "Pity." Instead she pointed at the wall. "Sit in the chair looking at the wall."

"I'm gonna lie on the bed for a nap instead."

"Eyes closed?"

He snorted. "Do you sleep with yours open?"

She turned her back rather than answer. She put in the plug and ran the water. The bed creaked as he climbed in. She glanced over her shoulder to see him on his side, facing away.

Her clothes hit the floor lightning fast, and she hopped into the water that was cold on one end then piping hot. She adjusted the temperature and quickly swirled with her feet to even out the burning spots. She sat with a splash, her knees bent since the tub didn't have the length to stretch.

"How's the water?" he suddenly asked.

"I thought you were sleeping."

"I will when your tub finishes filling. Do you have soap? Did you want me to go find some?"

"There's some jars on the ledge. Pretty sure at least one is soap."

He said nothing for a moment. The water rose, and she sighed as she luxuriated in the heat.

Then gasped as it suddenly turned biting-ass cold. She scrambled for the taps in a panic to stop it and found herself face to face with Quinn.

"What's wrong?" he asked.

"Cold water." She slowly cranked the handles and shut off the deluge. The remaining water remained warm at least.

"Oh." His gaze dropped only for a second before lifting. Was that ruddy color in his cheeks? "Do you need a towel to warm up?"

There were only inches apart, her leaning forward still, him crouched by the side of the tub. Yet suddenly their mouths were meshed together. Joined and yet sliding, a sensuous glide that hitched her breath and brought a shiver to her skin.

His hand slid into the water and cupped her mound, teasing her. Her hips thrust into his palm.

He groaned against her mouth. He dragged her out of the tub, into his lap, soaking himself in the process. His finger found her and slid in, leading her to gasp as she rode his hand in his lap. She uttered a sharp cry that he caught with his lips as she had a tiny orgasm.

It might have led to a bigger one if not for the sudden sharp rapping and the yell of someone below.

Erryn froze, and Quinn chuckled. "I think we just got told to behave."

The moment ended with her rising from his lap, suddenly chilly. She slid back into the warm waters and sighed as she sank down, submerging her head. Once she'd soaked her hair, she poured the contents of a vial into her hand and rubbed it until it lathered before applying it to her head.

By the time she'd rinsed and wiped her eyes enough to see, Quinn had changed his shirt to a soft plaid. He was putting on his jacket.

That led to her frowning. "Where are you going? I thought you were going to wait a while longer."

"Changed my mind."

"Gunner will be pissed if you get caught."

His teeth gleamed in his wide grin. "He will. But he also knows I'll most likely ignore his advice."

"Any ideas as to what you'll find?" As if to punctuate her query, a distant howl rose as twilight fell. The moon wasn't yet full, though. Did that mean they had at least one alpha who could shift on demand? Maybe more? It would be interesting to study if this non-pack still nominated alphas to positions of power.

"No clue, but this place is worth a look if only to get a better idea of numbers."

"Let me guess, you want me to stay here while you go prancing around."

"First off, I don't prance. I trot. And two, if I stay

here, we both know our lovely hostess will end up kicking us out in the middle of the night."

He had a point. "Go. Have fun. But try to not get caught. I doubt the rebels will look kindly upon a Cabal agent."

"They wouldn't dare harm me. The Cabal would retaliate."

"Would they?" she countered. "If you think that, then you don't know the Cabal well at all. As we discussed, they allowed this town to exist because it suits a purpose. If you're interfering with that plot, they'll let you die rather than veer from their course."

"You work for them and yet you don't trust them," he accused.

"Do you?"

"I think that, while somewhat rigid, they do the best they can to keep a wide and fractured web of Lycans from being eradicated."

"They do, but they could do better." Gunner was right. The world soon wouldn't be able to ignore evidence of their kind. And then what? The Cabal still insisted on hiding their heads in the sand. They really should be acting before they got caught with their wolves out.

"Easy for you to say. You can study Lycans all you want, but you'll never be one. Never feel that hunger. That push, pulse, and euphoria of becoming your wolf."

"And that kind of thinking is why things don't change." She swirled the cooling water with her hands.

She wasn't getting out until he left. "Shouldn't you be off spying?"

"I'm going," he exclaimed. "But first, if the old lady is still awake, I'm going to charm her into showing me some photo albums."

"Why would you care about her family?"

"Because she used to be mated to a Lycan, or did you somehow miss the scar on her neck or the fact she kept a stash of men's clothes?"

How had she missed a scar? "A bite mark doesn't mean they were married."

He snorted. "And you're supposed to be the smart one. Get some sleep. You obviously need it." He left, and she fled the bath before it got any chillier. The towel was old and worn but big enough to wrap around her.

In the pile of clothes given to her was a voluminous nightgown, the kind that somehow led to large families, and yet she'd never seen anything less sexy. It covered her head to toe, did nothing for her shape, but it was warm, the fleecy material cozy.

As she crawled into the bed, she wondered if Quinn remained downstairs talking to Velma. The reasoning behind it had her wondering if she, too, should get a peek. This town really provided an interesting contrast to the Lycans she'd observed in other societal structures. While all in a pack, each varied in how they conducted themselves. Some very loosely gathered and were barely family. Others built tight bonds.

Quinn for example. She could see the high regard he had for his pack and those in it. Those people were his brothers. And yet he had no issue gallivanting off across the world simply because the Cabal asked.

Her? She owed allegiance to no one, although she would lift a hand to help her mentor. He'd been a solid presence for her since he'd walked into that classroom to find her crying and bleeding, Joseph dead, still in his wolf shape. Erryn, her arms chewed, sobbing in shock.

Professor Frederick Monroe took one look and exhaled loudly. "This isn't good."

"I killed him. I didn't mean to." Erryn apologized, unable to look at the monster on the floor. Surely people would understand she'd killed in self-defense. She wasn't even sure how she'd created the gouges marring the wolf's body since she kept her nails blunt.

"You had a right to defend yourself. Joseph didn't give you a choice. But not everyone will see it like that."

She'd wrung her hands. "They'll put me in jail. I'll die."

"You're not going to jail," Professor Monroe replied harshly.

No, but she might die of rabies. Her arms throbbed, but not as badly as before. Did it mean she'd already lost too much blood? She should bind her wounds.

"Let's get you somewhere safe." He went to usher her out, but she glanced back at the body.

"If I leave, they'll think I'm guilty."

"No one will ever know this happened. I promise, I'll keep you safe."

And Professor Monroe had, but only because of his clout in the Cabal. Somehow, he'd convinced them to let her live. Taken her under his wing and treated her like a daughter. How she wished she could talk to him. Maybe he could make sense of this town.

The house had a silence to it, broken only by the occasional creak. The rustling of the thatched roof as rodents scurried.

The bed felt too big, the room too empty. She should have been used to being alone by now. But like a masochist, she couldn't help hoping for something else.

Someone.

Like Quinn.

9

QUINN DIDN'T WANT to leave that attic. At the same time, he felt an urge to flee.

Far as he could.

Being close to the doc was doing stuff to him. Stuff that scared the fuck out of him but also had him feeling more alive that he'd ever imagined.

It confused and led to him to clutch to any excuse to escape, and she didn't stop him. Thank fuck. He probably wouldn't have been able to say no had she asked.

He left the naked and tempting doc to her bath and headed down the stairs, being sure to close the hatch to their room. He had no way of locking it, and that gave him a moment of pause. Should he be leaving her? Protecting the doctor was his job.

But who would protect him from her allure?

He wouldn't go far, not to mention those targeting them shouldn't have tracked them here yet. It helped to know the town kept an eye on strangers. The moment they'd walked past that first house, he'd noticed the twitching of curtains, the casual glances from those out and about. They'd been noted. He had no doubt even now someone watched the house.

Good. That meant it wouldn't be easy for anyone to get in while he went poking around. The main floor showed no one in the kitchen or cozy living area, the door to a room smelling heavily of their hostess most likely indicated her bedchamber.

He didn't disturb her. He'd thrown the album excuse at Erryn as a means of escaping. It would be easier without his landlady noticing his departure. He slipped into the backyard, a place of thick shadows. No sliver of moon, nor even a hint of stars tonight. The moist and heavy air indicated rain in the forecast. As if thinking it brought it down, droplets began to fall, a curtain that soaked and chilled, but it also muffled scent and sound. With the gloom, he relied on his senses, much like a certain Skywalker. He didn't close his eyes, but he did tune in with his ears, even his skin. Variations in the air often provided all the warning needed.

He didn't sense anyone, the only life being that of the cat currently stalking a mouse. Rather than exit to the front, he slipped from Velma's yard to the next-door neighbor. Two windows overlooked the yard. The one spilling light from slight cracks had a thick curtain pulled over it. He stealthily moved past it, tiptoeing through a garden so as not to crush the stalks struggling against a rapidly creeping fall.

Only once he'd gone to the very end of the block did he exit onto a road, dark and wet. No streetlights shone. A waste of electricity and cost to maintain when a good portion of the town could navigate the dark.

He stood and waited for a second, surprised he'd not yet spotted a tail. Gunner hadn't seemed very trusting. Quinn still couldn't believe they'd run into his old army and Lycan brother. It had been a while since he'd seen his quasi friend. At least he looked better.

The last time he'd seen Gunner, the man's gaunt appearance indicated either he wasn't eating or an illness. And not necessarily the bodily kind. Add in long, wild hair, feverish eyes, along with unhinged ranting and Quinn had worried for Gunner, even as his brother refused all help.

Instead, with a vehement conviction, he declared, "I'm so close to finding a cure." He'd truly believed he could be rid of it. Apparently, he'd finally realized he couldn't and come to peace with it. Kind of.

Gunner appeared to have a hate-on for the Cabal. For some reason, he thought of the Cabal as his enemy. Which was fine. He could have his belief. He obviously wasn't alone, given the size of this town. A town flourishing, thinking they flouted Cabal rule. In reality? The doc had it right when she said they allowed this place to exist. The Cabal could crush it at any moment if needed, meaning they had a use for this town hidden in Europe. A place where certain

Cabal rules didn't apply. Like the snipping of a guy's junk.

Gunner had lied when Erryn asked about babies. Someone else might not have caught the flicker, but Quinn did. There were people getting preggers and having Lycan children. If he got lucky tonight, he'd have some names and addresses to visit tomorrow. And they'd find out if Erryn's claim was true. Did they have Lycan females?

As he headed for the main street, he finally acquired a shadow. He slowed his pace to drawl, "Took you long enough."

Gunner stepped into the open with an annoyed scowl. "I told you to stay inside."

"I needed a breath of fresh air."

"Then open a window. The town's not safe at night"

"I'm a big boy. I think I can handle it."

"Then you're an idiot," Gunner snapped.

"Care to tell me why a grown-ass man can't take a nice evening constitutional?" As they argued, he happened to notice movement inside the bell tower of the church. "Is that a fucking sniper?" The muzzle of the rifle rested on a tripod on the lip of a window.

"Yeah, but he's more an early warning system than anything. The monster moves too fast for him to get a proper bead."

The claim arched Quinn's brow. He was finally getting somewhere. "What monster?"

"The one that snatches the unwary. And before

you ask, no, we haven't killed it yet. Fucker is too goddammed fast. Doesn't help it hits at random. Sometimes it's months in between attacks. Other times, it strikes within days or weeks."

"How many monsters?"

"Just the one that we know of."

Quinn shoved his hands into his pockets. "Do you have a description?"

"Walks on two legs, but they're bent, like haunches. Hairy all over. We've got some blurry pics. It only comes at night. Loves shitty weather."

"Does it have wings?" Quinn asked. He wondered for a second if the monster from Brock's shop and this one were related.

"Fucking wings? Why the fuck would you even ask that?"

"Because you're not the only one dealing with a monster. You should talk to Brock," Quinn suggested.

"I'd rather not. Last I heard, the man services vampires." Gunner didn't hide his disdain.

"He's your friend. And a job is a job. You don't hold the Cabal against me."

"That's what you think," Gunner muttered.

"Talk to him. He's got monster issues too. Not sure if they're related, but it can't hurt to compare notes."

As they resumed walking, Gunner managed an awkward, "Your doctor lady seems nice."

That had him barking with laughter. "Doc ain't nice, but she is sexy, and smart, and—" He almost said, "Mine."

"She must be smart. I didn't think the Cabal liked working with humans."

"Some of them are coming around to the fact we need to coexist."

"Too slowly," Gunner argued. "The world is a different place. People aren't superstitious like before. This town is proof we could live in the open."

"A small town in the middle of nowhere is one thing. You know some will never accept us in their midst." One had to only look at the vying religious factions and political groups to see the world was more polarized and split than ever.

"There are always dissenters. It's time all Lycans lived free of the Cabal."

"That sounds all fine and dandy except that there are some that need others making the rules for them. That require a firm guiding hand. And what of the vulnerable that need their protection?"

Gunner stared at him. "You're taking their side."

"I'm saying that different people need different things."

"The Cabal isn't even elected. Why should anyone listen to them?"

"Because they've kept us safe for centuries. Because they want Lycans to thrive."

A sneer pulled at Gunner's lips. "I swear you like being their lap dog. Look at you, here arguing with me in the rain instead of snuggled in the bosom of your pack."

"This has fuck all to do with the Cabal. I'm here

because of Erryn." The truth slipped out. A truth he'd not been ready for. Quinn might have been given the job to stick close to her side, but bit by bit, it was becoming something else.

"Ah yes, *Erryn.*" Said with a tone that Quinn didn't like. "There's something off about your doctor. Her scent is wrong."

His nostrils flared. "I happen to think she smells perfect." Especially since she'd lost that horrible perfume she used to wear.

"You are so smitten. It's gross." Gunner shook his head as if in despair.

"I am not."

"Really? So if I tell you that Velma lost her granddaughter to a monster less than a year ago in the very same room you're staying in, you aren't going to suddenly go racing back to her side?"

His blood turned cold. "What? How could a monster even get inside? There's only the one window, and it's not exactly accessible."

Disdainful laughter. "Have you seen the roof?"

The implication—danger to his doc—almost had him bolting. Only the taunting kept him rooted in place. "Erryn will be fine. She's not useless like most."

"Grand praise coming from you."

"Why are being such a dick?" Quinn suddenly asked. "Like seriously? What the fuck did I ever do to you to deserve you acting like a prick?"

Gunner's lips flattened. "You're the one who mistakenly thinks we're friends."

"I thought we were more like brothers."

A bitter laugh bubbled from Gunner. "Family. Yes, that would explain our dysfunction. Brothers not by choice but by blood. Do you ever think of Scarecrow?" The name they'd all used when speaking of the man who changed them.

"Not much these days, no."

"I still have nightmares of leaving Scarecrow behind," Gunner admitted softly.

"He told us to because he didn't want us wasting our strength on a dead man."

"Only he wasn't dead when we left. Maybe we could have saved him if we'd brought him with us."

"We could barely hold ourselves upright and you wanted us to drag the corpse of another?"

Gunner's expression pinched. "Leave no man behind."

The guilt hit Quinn hard, but he wasn't about to admit how that moment had often haunted. "Too late for regrets."

"Too late for a lot of things," Gunner declared harshly. "There is no going back. No making things right."

The tormented words reminded Quinn of Gunner before they became prisoners and received the Lycan bite. Once upon a time, Gunner was engaged to his high school sweetheart, a young woman whom he adored more than anything. They never did marry.

After they were discharged, Quinn only once asked Gunner what happened. He'd gotten a low, "*She couldn't marry a monster."* Quinn had to wonder if Gunner ever got over the heartache.

He changed the subject to one more interesting to him. This town. "You have elections to choose a leader?"

"Leaders," Gunner corrected. "We have a committee of five that serve three years at a time with a person from each tiered age group representing."

"Sounds complicated."

"We wanted to ensure everyone had a voice from the young to the old."

"And is it working?"

Gunner shrugged, hands shoved in his pockets. The rain tapered to a heavy mist that swirled, making it even harder to see more than a few paces at a time. "So far it seems to be doing more good than harm. They make rules, the people follow them. Even like them well enough that two of the oldest townspeople, Dmitri, who is Lycan, and his wife, Joella, have been reelected each time they put their name in the hat."

"And what of troublemakers?" The rot that could kill a peaceful balance.

"We don't tolerate them."

"So you kick them out?"

Gunner's lips flattened. "Depends on their crime."

A dick would have pointed out Gunner's committee was just as brutal as the Cabal when it came to ruling, but Quinn preferred to keep the peace.

"Are you happy here?" Not exactly the most discreet question and he half expected Gunner to tell him to fuck off. Back in his military days, there would have been much mocking of showing feelings. He'd grown out of it. Mostly. It still felt weird asking.

Gunner shrugged. "It's a place that doesn't suck as bad as others." He paused and asked, much too casually, "Why is your woman interested in babies? You'd think as a doctor working for the Cabal, she'd know it wasn't possible."

"She delivered one not long ago." Quinn dropped the truth bomb, and Gunner didn't even stumble.

"Nice try. We both know the Cabal would never allow it."

"Think again. They did allow it, and a boy was born. Healthy. Not showing any Lycan genes," Quinn revealed, waiting to see if Gunner would do the same.

"They don't at that age." It was so softly muttered Quinn almost didn't catch it.

"You're not surprised," Quinn accused.

"Birth control sometimes fails. Vasectomies don't always last forever. And sometimes the wolf doesn't emerge right away after a bite. In a community this size, accidents happen."

"And when they do, then what?"

"We don't hide the truth from the pregnant mothers," Gunner stated. "Just like we're honest with the odds. Many will not survive. Sometimes we get lucky and can save the mother and child. Other times, we only manage one."

"I assume you are keeping them out of moonlight?"

Gunner nodded. "And giving them old wives'

concoctions that are supposed to stop the babies from becoming violent in the womb and shredding their mothers."

"Erryn managed to stop it from happening in Ulric's mate. It was close a few times, but the boy is healthy."

"Then they were lucky. I've seen too many tears when it fails. Poor Velma. The baby made it, but her daughter..." Gunner's lips turned down.

"Yeah, I don't know if I'd risk it. Good thing I never wanted any runts of my own." But Quinn had to wonder after seeing Ulric with his son, the softness of his expression, the fierceness of the love reflected.

"I used to want a half-dozen with—" Gunner shook his head, his eyes shut, and cleared his throat. "Doesn't matter anymore. That ship has sailed."

Given his friend appeared more open, Quinn had to ask. "Can you help Erryn and hook her up with some of the success stories? And knowing her, she'll want to know all about the failures too."

That caused Gunner to snap from melancholy to angry suspicion. "Why the fuck would I do that? She'll tell the Cabal."

"It's something—"

A scream interrupted their discussion, shrill and close by. Long legs sprinted as Quinn and Gunner headed for the noise. They veered around a corner in time to spot someone struggling with a monster. A young girl by the looks of it. She pummeled at the hairy beast while what could only be her mother slapped it with a broom. A body of a male lay prone on the ground, senseless or dead.

Another furry shape shot from the house, a grizzled wolf, who tackled into the monster, snapping and gnashing its teeth at the flesh. Had to be an alpha. Only they could change without the full moon.

"That's Jarrod, one of the committee leaders," Gunner shouted. "And that's his daughter. We have to help."

No fucking shit.

A smart Quinn remained armed with a gun taken from the train attackers. He lifted it now but couldn't get a clear shot.

Fuck.

Gunner went left. Quinn headed right, tucking the weapon away so that he could grab at an arm, which proved to be hairy and wiry, also very strong. He couldn't get it to bend. The monster uttered a shriek of rage as all three Lycans, one actually wolf, pulled its limbs in different directions.

The cry received a reply, and Quinn barely had time to turn before a new threat was upon him.

Hands tipped in claws gripped him and tried to hold him still to be chomped by a slavering jaw with jagged teeth. Fuck that! They tussled on the ground, rolling and grunting as the new monster sought to tear out his throat. Quinn barely managed to keep his face from getting eaten. Had his nose been a smidge longer...

He managed to wedge a knee between their bodies

enough to launch the fucker. The monster recovered quickly, but so did Quinn. He pulled the gun and fired at close range, and the monster couldn't avoid the bullet. It punched into its chest and through it, causing it to waver on its feet, which was when Quinn put the second bullet in its brain. Then a third for good measure.

Then he whirled in time to see the grizzled wolf ripping out the throat of the other monster, pinned to the ground by Gunner. As for the woman, she sobbed over the girl.

His gaze returned to bounce between the two monstrous bodies.

Two.

More howling exploded in the distance, and Quinn glared at Gunner. "That's more than one."

Flesh pale, his blood brother replied, "I think we're under attack."

And Erryn was alone.

The thought sent Quinn running, hoping he wasn't too late.

10

SLEEPING PROVED IMPOSSIBLE. Erryn blamed Quinn for that. She kept wondering where he was, what he was doing, did he need help? He'd probably say no. Stupid macho guy.

A guy who'd made her tingle then ran away.

Coward.

She wasn't much better. She could have argued. Seduced. Done all kinds of things to keep him. Except for crying. She didn't do tears to get her way.

What she also didn't do? Obey orders very well. He'd told her to stay in the room. The room didn't have anything to drink, and she wasn't about to shove her head under the tap in the sink.

Wearing her giant muumuu nightgown, she tucked the loose fabric between her legs best she could and climbed down the ladder stairs. The kitchen proved easy to find, along with a kettle and some milk.

The wall held a landline phone, the kind with a

hard plastic casing and square buttons to push. Just a step above rotary. Not secure at all, meaning she didn't even bother using it. A reassuring chat with Fred would have to wait until she got her hands on a burner phone.

As Erryn set the flame on the stove to boil water, Velma entered the kitchen wearing a matching night-gown, her gray hair plaited. She spotted the kettle and proceeded to fetch them mugs as well as some honey and milk.

In companionable silence, they waited for the water to boil and the tea—a mint blend good for calming the nerves— to steep in a mug. A dollop of honey sweetened, and the cream cooled.

After a deep gulp, Velma smacked her lips. "Good."

"Very good." Then because Erryn had nothing to lose, she said, "Do you have children?"

Velma cocked her head.

"Babies? You?" She pointed and mimed rocking.

Velma's face took on a sad cast. "Baby. Gone." She rose from her seat, and for a moment, Erryn felt chagrin at sending her fleeing, only the woman returned with an album.

Hunh.

Velma set it down and pointed, saying names that had no meaning but belonged to various people. But the one that got the saddest introduction, "Daughter. Nadja." A beautiful girl that grew in the pictures, until she was a woman with a swelling belly.

And then Nadja was gone in the images, replaced by baby Svetlana.

No need to ask what happened. Death in childbirth remained all too common even with modern medicine.

The album had plenty of pictures of the baby girl with a bright smile and fat golden curls. She was pictured riding on her grandfather's shoulders, a burly man with impressive whiskers. Having her first birthday with Grandma Velma holding a cake. Riding a trike. The three of them together forming a happy family.

With a large dog that only appeared rarely.

Wait, that wasn't a dog. "Is that a wolf?" Then to be sure Velma understood, Erryn pointed to the dog first and howled. "Awoo."

Velma nodded and chattered a few words before pointing to her husband and saying clearly, "Dead."

"How did he die?"

Her lips turned down as she turned to the last page, two newspaper clippings. One was an obituary notice for Velma's husband. The other a blurry picture of Svetlana and a blob of text, but it took the second picture, showing a hole in a roof and the bedroom upstairs before Erryn put it together. Something had attacked the baby. The grandfather must have tried to save her and died.

"I'm so sorry."

Velma's head dipped. As Erryn reached out a rare consoling hand to her shoulder, she heard a thump.

Both she and Velma glanced up to the ceiling. Without a word, Velma rose and headed for the counter. Erryn got to her feet more slowly. No need to panic. Most likely it was Quinn returning. Tell that to her gut, which insisted otherwise, especially since seeing that clipping. Had something come through the roof again? Quinn had been right when he said the town had secrets. After all, who the hell broke through a roof to take a child?

It reminded her of Brock's garage when that monster chose the roof as its point of access. Surely those creatures hadn't followed them here.

Slowly, Erryn eased out of the kitchen to see the door to the street shut. The hatch at the top of the ladder remained open. She heard a creak overhead. Someone, or something, was definitely up there. Should she call out? It might be Quinn. If not, though, any sound she made would give them warning of her location. Not the best idea given she had no weapon.

I need something to fight with. The kitchen had knives. As she thought about arming herself, something literally pounced from the attic room, ignoring the ladder steps, and slammed into her.

She reeled at the impact, and that saved her, as the swiping claws missed their intended eviscerating slash. She hit a wall, bounced, and bolted away from the monster into the kitchen, the only place offering a second exit.

She narrowly avoided being impaled on the knife Velma held in one hand. The other wielded a frying pan. Brave and foolish, given she didn't stand a chance against a powerful beast.

But Velma didn't care. She screamed and ran for the monster, who batted her aside as if she were nothing. It advanced on Erryn, its eyes practically glowing with malevolence.

"What are you?" she muttered aloud, noticing its resemblance and differences from the monster they'd seen in the garage. For one, its nose was more pronounced, the face longer, and this one had no wings on its back. A scraggly-looking wolfman who wanted to eat her.

Erryn grabbed and threw everything in reach. Honey pot. Mugs. Kettle. It kept dodging and advancing, slowly, as if enjoying itself. The door she'd been retreating toward didn't open when she yanked. Locked!

The creature threw itself at her as she struggled to undo its clasp. She threw up an arm at the last second, and teeth clamped onto her arm right through the thin fabric of the gown. Erryn grunted rather than screamed. This wasn't her first time being mauled.

The thing growled as it shook its head. She let her arm go limp rather than fight and tear the gouges deeper. Trying to tear off her limb kept the monster busy while her free hand searched for a weapon.

Velma was the one to find the right tool. She grabbed the poker by the kitchen hearth. The beast never saw the tip coming. Velma punctured it in the leg, causing it to squeal and drop Erryn's arm. She wasted no time ducking and grabbing the bobbing poker, ripping it from flesh.

Erryn held the pointed tip in front of her, threatening the beast. "Back off," she growled, as if it could understand.

The monster uttered a hiss, its mouth ringed in her blood. It would regret that bite. Its flesh rippled. The monster howled in a way to lift the hair on her body. It shook its head and pulled at the hair on its chest as if in pain.

It lunged, and she jabbed with the poker. The monster recoiled.

"What's wrong? Not so fun when you're not the only one who can draw blood?" she taunted. Anger coursed through her, along with a burning pain from the site of the bite. She was getting really tired of monsters taking her for an easy snack.

With a cry of rage, she threw herself at the beast, swinging the poker, hitting it while screaming. Velma, a mourning mother seeking vengeance, joined her with a large kitchen knife. Flesh ribboned. Blood spattered. And a monster regretted its attack.

By the time Quinn burst in, Gunner on his heels, the beast was dead in a pool of its own blood, its head hanging by a sliver of flesh while its gore covered Erryn.

Looking fiercely happy, Velma tapped the hilt of her knife to her chest and ululated. A wife and grandmother satisfied with her vengeance.

"What the fuck happened?" Gunner exclaimed while Quinn scanned her.

"Monster attacked. We killed it. Seems kind of obvious," she said with a roll of her eyes.

"Those monsters are practically impossible to take down," Gunner insisted.

"Guess we got lucky," she stated.

"More like this one was sickly," Gunner noted, dropping to his haunches by the mishappen body. Flesh showed in spots. One of the paws had two fingers, in jarring contrast to the claws.

She glanced away as Quinn sidled close.

"You're hurt?" Quinn remarked a little too softly. He appeared stiff and angry. Probably because he'd not been able to pull a hero.

"I'm fine." She eyed her bloodied nightgown. "Although I think I need another bath."

"A bath?" He almost choked saying it.

"Excuse me a moment."

She fled the room, heading quickly for the ladder and up into a room that had a gaping hole in the thatched roof. For a moment she paused. What if another beast came through? She had no weapon.

"Clean yourself off. I'll keep watch." Quinn had followed.

She moved into the room, allowing him to finish the climb. "Are there more do you think?"

"Who the fuck knows," he grumbled. "Gunner was under the impression the town only had a single monster to worry about. The one you killed makes three dead tonight alone. Gunner and I handled a pair outside. And I heard more yelling farther off in town."

She pursed her lips. "We should go see if anyone needs help."

"There are enough people in town to handle it. My concern is you."

"I told you I'm fine."

"You're fucking bleeding." Finally, his calm snapped.

"You don't say. If you don't mind, I'd like to wash off."

He didn't turn around, and she arched a brow.

"A little privacy?"

"I've already seen it." He crossed his arms.

"You are the most stubborn and annoying man."

"Ditto. Let's go. Show me the boo-boo."

"Fuck off," she growled as she tugged at her gown, pulling it upward, the voluminous material getting tangled around her head, leaving her exposed to his gaze.

She finally managed to toss the gown aside, the heavy material having done a good job of protecting Erryn from the blood spattered in the attack. With it gone, though, she could no longer hide the oozing mess on her arm.

Quinn uttered an eerie sound as he grumbled, "It bit you."

"Yeah. But don't worry. I won't start howling at the moon." She turned from him and turned on the water, trying to pretend she wasn't naked and bending over.

Did he look? Did she want him to look? Kind of a shit time for her to think it, but it distracted from the throb in her flesh.

"Don't you get in that tub. We need to disinfect that bite mark. Fuck only knows what kind of germs that thing had in its mouth. Last thing you want is a nasty infection."

"It won't get infected," she opined as she slid into the chilly tub, leaving the plug out and choosing to rinse her bloody hands and face. Then she let the water run over her mangled arm. Another scar. Yay.

"Why are you being so fucking calm about this?" he yelled.

She eyed him. "This is not the first or even second time this has happened."

"What's that supposed to mean?"

"I'm irresistible." When his face remained blankly uncomprehending, she expanded. "My scent does something to Lycans. Makes them go a little crazy if they're shifted. Or so we figured out after the second time I got bit."

"The first being the attack at the university," he murmured in slow understanding.

"Lucky for me, the Cabal member who rescued me helped to find a way for me to avoid smelling like a tasty treat."

"That hideous scent you wear." His nose wrinkled.

"Does the job and usually repels unwanted attention. I wonder if it would have worked with the monster downstairs," she mused aloud.

He glanced at the hole in the roof then her. "You weren't easy prey. It came after you specifically."

She rolled her shoulders. "What can I say? Apparently, I'm also irresistible to monsters."

"Not funny," he huffed, seething with anger.

"It's my reality," she said, placing her damaged arm under the gush of cold water. She'd not turned on the hot yet, as she wanted to numb her flesh.

He dropped to his haunches and leaned to grab the gown she'd stripped. He ripped a clean section from it. She held out her dripping arm, the punctures barely oozing, and let him bind it. Let him feel as if he did something. Why not? It was a novelty to have someone show her that kind of care.

He eyed her. "You missed a spot." He used his thumb to rub her jawline. He rinsed his hand then returned it to cup her face. "You're awfully calm about this."

"I've have had more than a decade to get used to my situation."

"I don't like it."

"Then a good thing it's not your problem."

He rose, rigid, his jaw as tight as his body. She half expected him to stomp off in a snit. Instead, he grabbed a towel and held it out, waiting.

She stood and stepped from the tub into the waiting rough fabric. He wound it around her, trapping her arms, before lifting her and carrying her to the bed. He tucked her under the covers and lay beside her.

"Shouldn't you be helping Gunner with the body?" she asked.

"His monster. His town. He can handle it. You need me more than him."

She wanted to deny it, and yet cradled against him, she wouldn't deny enjoying his warmth. "We should probably find another place to sleep. That hole in the roof will suck if it rains again."

"I'm more worried about other things coming through." He scowled at it then sighed. "Sorry, Doc, but we're changing rooms."

"To where?"

"Living room for the night. We'll find another place to stay in the morning."

She rolled from the bed, slapping at his hands. "I can walk."

"I'm more worried about climbing with that arm."

"I'll be fine." How many times would she say that before he finally listened?

"I'll go down first just in case. But first..." He snagged the mattress from the frame, not the kind made of springs and foam but more like a giant pillow-case stuffed with feathers. Old-school bedding. He tossed it down the hatch and then leaped down after it.

She sighed. He was taking the coddling a touch too far. Then again, she'd not counted on the difficulty in climbing wrapped in a towel.

When her feet tangled, almost dumping her, his hands were there to steady then pluck her from the ladder. He set her on her feet, and she pursed her lips as he carried the mattress into the living room. He then headed up the ladder and tossed down the blankets and pillows. She grabbed them before he could and set them on the bed.

As she turned around, Gunner appeared, a hairy body over his shoulder, looking more mishappen than she recalled and missing its head. The plastic bag in his hand was about the right size for one, though.

"Worried it will rise again?" she quipped.

Gunner glanced in her direction. "Given how tough these bastards are, it's probably best we don't take chances."

Good point.

Gunner headed out the front door, and Quinn glanced at her. "I'll be back in a second. I want to talk to Gunner."

She headed into the kitchen to find Velma scrubbing at the blood, muttering. She glanced up at Erryn and frowned. She chattered quickly as she rose to her feet. She went to her bedroom and returned with a fresh gown.

"Thank you." She managed to get the gown on without flashing Velma. The damp towel got whisked away.

As Erryn sipped on a fresh cup of tea, the men returned, murmuring in a low tone. She caught only a word here and there. *Dead. Two missing. Hunt.* Meaning some monsters had escaped.

She expected Quinn to join his friend in tracking them down. The front door closed, clicked as it locked, and Quinn appeared in the kitchen. He checked her over before accepting the cup of tea Velma handed him.

The woman dumped her bloody bucket in the sink and rinsed her rag before uttering a short, "Bed. Bye."

Velma left, and Erryn eyed Quinn. "I'm surprised you're not out with your friend looking for more of those monsters." A terrible word to use and yet what she'd fought didn't look anything like a Lycan.

"And leave you alone? Not a chance, Doc."

"I think I've proven I can handle myself."

"You have and not the point. I had one job, and I failed miserably. It won't happen again."

She cocked her head. "You couldn't know I'd be attacked."

"Given the trip we've had so far?" He snorted. "I should have predicted it, and you almost paid the price."

"God save me from guys with a macho-man complex." She rolled her eyes as she took her cup to the sink for a rinse.

"Why is it so hard for you to accept help?"

"Why is it so hard for you to realize I don't want it?"

"Too bad. The Cabal ordered me to watch over you, and that's what I'm going to do."

"Do you always obey?"

"Don't you?"

She pursed her lips. "Depends on the circumstances."

"Ditto. Now, if we're done discussing my ethics, let's get some sleep."

"Sleep?" She snorted. "I'm a little too wired for that."

"Try." He led the way the cramped living room and their bed wedged between the couch and wall. His shirt came off first, revealing a body that had her averting her gaze, even as she wanted nothing more than to stare.

Before he could smell her interest, she ducked under the thick cover and heard rather than saw him stripping off his trousers before sliding into the bed on the floor with her. The mattress width and the fact it squished meant they ended up touching in the middle. Not just touching, he spooned her as if it were natural, his arm over her waist, palm on her belly. She snuggled into him, feeling herself relax, but sleep lingered out of reach.

"Where did Gunner take the body?" she asked.

"No idea."

"I should have told your friend to put it on ice so I could autopsy it."

"I'm sure you're not the only one who'll want to examine it."

"There was something not right about it," she muttered.

"No shit. It smelled majorly wrong too."

"Will you contact Gunner in the morning and find out where they took it so I can take a peek?"

"I will find a shovel and dig it up myself if I have to."

She smiled. "It pains me to admit you're a nicer guy than I gave you credit for."

"Don't tell anyone. I have a reputation to uphold."

And she needed to remind herself that getting close was a bad idea.

11

QUINN WOKE the moment Erryn slid from their bed on the floor. He said nothing as she fled, listening as she headed cautiously up the ladder stairs. The pipes rattled when she flushed and gurgled as she ran water and freshened up. He left her to do her things in private but ready to act if he heard anything untoward. Given dawn had cracked, he didn't expect much.

By the time she clambered down the stairs, he sat in the kitchen holding a mug of coffee strong enough to make him sprout hair all over. In front of him sat a plate of eggs, sausage, and roasted potatoes, making him drool.

Raised with manners, Quinn jumped to his feet at her appearance. Her face was still damp, and she was dressed in the clothes Velma provided. Clean but over-sized. He'd see about getting her some stuff that fit when they went out.

He held out a chair in the cramped space. She glanced at him and murmured, "Thanks."

Only once she was seated with a plate of her own did he dig in. But their hostess didn't.

Velma bustled around with a smile. Killing the monster that might have been the one to attack her granddaughter and husband must have felt good. The kitchen showed no sign of the carnage from the night before and smelled faintly of bleach.

A knock at the door had Quinn standing, ready to act, only to relax as Gunner let himself in, calling out, "It's just me. Morning."

Velma didn't bat an eye and set another plate.

Quinn sat back down. "You're here bright and early. Need a hand with something?"

"I was hoping to borrow your doctor friend." Gunner looked at Erryn.

Despite not having a good reason, Quinn didn't like it one bit.

Erryn finished chewing a bite of toast before saying, "I'm assuming this has to do with the beast."

"We'd like your opinion on it."

"We who?" Quinn growled.

"The committee. There are things about the creatures we killed last night that are raising some questions. Given the doctor's area of expertise, we could use her insight."

"What kind of observations are we talking about?" Erryn asked.

"For one, the beast you killed appeared to be mid-shift."

"Shift?" Quinn caught the word and repeated it. "You're saying they're Lycan?"

"No, but I do believe they're related to us." Gunner's lips twisted in disgust.

"Those things weren't wolves," Quinn insisted.

"But they had the characteristics," Erryn mused aloud. "Fur. Fangs. The noise it made."

"It walked on two legs, had hands, not paws," Quinn countered.

"Haven't you heard of the wolfman?" Erryn offered with a lift of a brow.

Quinn's lips pressed tight, and Gunner jumped in. "Are we going to argue about this all morning or check it out?"

"I'm going with her."

"I assumed you would," Gunner replied almost mockingly.

"Give me a moment to help Velma clean up." Erryn went to remove her plate, and Velma snatched it, chattering rapidly.

Gunner nodded before saying, "She says to go and that she'll have the roof mended before tonight."

"She still wants us staying here?" Erryn sounded surprised.

"Says she owes you a debt for helping her avenge her family."

"What if another monster returns?" Erryn argued. "She could have been killed."

"We won't be surprised again." Gunner's grim pronouncement.

They set out on foot, the morning bright and sunny if cool. Despite it being daytime, Quinn found his head swiveling side to side on high alert.

Not so Doc. She strolled along, casual as you could please, and full of questions. "How long have you been dealing with monsters?" A question directed at Gunner.

"A few years. Although last night was the first time we ever saw more than one at once. Was never more shocked than when that second beast pounced while we were taking care of the first." Gunner shook his head.

"How many casualties?"

"Last night or overall?" Gunner replied.

"Both," Erryn demanded.

"It was a bad one last night. We lost a young boy trying to protect a girl. She and her father suffered injuries but survived. A mother across town died trying to protect her child. We've yet to locate the toddler." Gunner's lips turned down.

"Did they not flee on foot?" Quinn asked.

"So you'd think, and yet they have a way of wiping their scent and disappearing."

"I didn't think it rained that hard last night," Quinn murmured.

"I'm aware it makes no sense." A low admission by Gunner. "Their scent is distinctive. We should be able to find them. But no matter who we send on the hunt, we come up empty-handed."

"Maybe because it's only unfamiliar when they're wolfmen. What if you lose them because their trail becomes something familiar?" Erryn mused softly.

"Are you trying to imply something?" Gunner asked.

"Just thinking aloud. There has to be a reason why their trail dead-ends. They got into a vehicle and moved elsewhere." She ticked off fingers. "They have a way of masking it."

"Not sure how since they weren't carrying any vials of perfume," drawled Quinn.

"A shift changes a person's smell."

"No one in this town would betray us."

"Said every person ever betrayed." On this, Quinn actually agreed with Erryn. Given the ease the monsters came in, took, and left, it would be crazy to not contemplate the fact they might have a few traitors amongst them.

"I won't believe it," a stubborn Gunner insisted. "If that we true, we'd have had three missing folk last night. But everyone is accounted for. And those not sleeping in their houses last night were on legitimate business."

"Pity because that means these monsters, as you call them, are smarter than you, seeing how well they poached your village."

Quinn almost winced at Erryn's savage delivery.

"They're wily," Gunner defended. "They only

attack at night, often when the weather is damp and unfavorable for tracking. In between their ambushes, we've combed the environs, looking for a trail, a scent, anything. It's like they vanish into thin air." Gunner rolled his shoulders.

"Which is impossible," Erryn interjected. "And yet you won't see the obvious. So let's move on. Why do they attack? You'd think if it was for food, they'd seek out easier prey."

"Aren't they, though? They've been going after young girls and not the men," Gunner huffed.

"Which is still rather brazen. What kind of security do you have?" she asked.

"We have someone in the church tower each night, plus random houses will have someone watching."

"That doesn't sound like much."

"A few of us patrol the streets, too."

"It doesn't sound very organized. What's your committee folk doing during all this? What have they done to counter the attacks?"

Gunner's lips almost went to a hair wide he pressed them so tight.

"Well?" she prodded.

"Not much," Gunner said through gritted teeth.

"I see." Nothing else, and yet so damned powerful Quinn almost applauded her subtle mastery, as Gunner spilled it all.

"They've mostly advocated for barricading ourselves at night."

"They don't want you to fight back?" Quinn

blurted out.

"Most of the folks in town aren't fighters. Just regular people who turn furry," Gunner explained, his shoulders lifting and dropping. "They don't know how to defend themselves, let alone take on those wolfmen."

"They are not wolfmen," Quinn grumbled.

"Maybe they are, and they're the next level for Lycan." Erryn didn't help him at all.

"That would imply they're as smart or smarter than us. I fought one. They're animals."

"So are you," she reminded. "Imagine, with your current abilities and intellect, plus the parts of the wolf that make you strong, what would that make you?"

"A monster." Gunner dipped his head.

"But you'd still be the same person," Quinn argued.

"He knows that and yet wants to wallow," Erryn opined, crossing the street that held no traffic.

Gunner almost fell stepping off the curb. "I do not wallow."

"You do. Don't care. That's not why I'm here."

"Maybe you're one of the monsters." Gunner sulked.

She snorted. "Only when on my period."

The red in Gunner's cheeks had Quinn biting the inside of his mouth to avoid laughing.

Then, while she had him, she said once more, "There is no way the monsters are working without help. A town this size should have seen something."

"People are sleeping usually."

Her lips turned down. "Keep making excuses. After all, what's a few more lives in the grand scheme of things?" She had a bitter edge to her words.

Quinn had to wonder if she thought of the Cabal. More and more it appeared as if the Cabal had been keeping secrets, at least about this town. No way they didn't know of the wolfmen and the Lycan births. The question being, was it all of them or simply a few covering up events in Gherdeal?

How much did they panic when they realized Doc's destination after giving her permission to seek out Lycan babies? Apparently enough to try and have her killed before she arrived.

Rather than give in to the brewing anger over possible Cabal perfidy, Quinn returned to something Gunner said earlier. "You mentioned they took a child. The one we fought last night also appeared to be trying to abduct that girl we saved."

"Because that's what they usually do. They sneak in, kill those who stand in their way, steal someone, then leave."

"And you don't recover the abducted?" Erryn clarified.

Gunner shook his head.

"What about bodies? Find any of those?" Quinn boldly asked despite it being morbid.

"We can't even give them a proper burial. It's been demoralizing. We've lost people over it. More than a dozen this year, which is huge in a place this size." His shoulders slumped.

145

Erryn frowned. "Why come into town, though? If they are acting on animal instinct, then a place this size would usually be avoided by predators."

"They were hungry," Quinn stated.

"Seems like it would have been simpler to hunt the edges of the town," she suggested.

She had a good point. Quinn pursed his lips. "We were almost in the heart last night when the attack happened."

"And Velma's place is pretty central too. So these wolfmen skipped a bunch of places because they were looking for something specific. What's attracting them? What do all those people have in common?"

"They have all been female." Gunner pointed out the most obvious clue.

"And young?" Quinn offered. "The girl we saved last night was a teenager. And the kid that was taken even younger."

"So it's not a specific age then," Erryn mused aloud, and then she made a leap. "Were those taken Lycan-born?"

Gunner stumbled before managing a hurried, "Don't be ridiculous."

"I really wish you wouldn't lie," Erryn chided. "I already know you've had some successful births."

"Whoever said that to you lied." Gunner's stiff reply came with an angry side-eye in Quinn's direction.

He raised his hands. "Don't blame me. She found out on her own because some of your people sent in samples to those online DNA places. Not exactly bright of them if you wanted to keep it secret."

A glaring Gunner led to Quinn grumbling, "It ain't my fault those kids were dumb."

"Now that we've gotten that out of the way, how about you try being honest so I can properly help?" Erryn tartly added.

Uttering a heavy sigh, Gunner replied, "We have some Lycan children."

"How many Lycan-born do you have in this town?"

"I don't know."

Erryn canted her head. "Well, let's see. Your town is older than the ten years you mentioned. I saw Velma's pictures of Nadja growing up in that same house. And she had to be at least sixteen or older before she died."

"Seventeen. The baby survived. She didn't." He ducked his head.

"The father?"

"Never came forth. Mostly likely because he'd have been killed by her father. Nadja claimed she didn't remember who it was. She'd been drinking at a party," Gunner explained.

"I'm going to assume he was Lycan," Erryn stated.

"Yes." A short, bitten-off word.

"Which brings me back to my original point. The town is old enough to have seen the births of several Lycan babies. More than anyone thought possible."

"Not as many as you're implying," was Gunner's scowled reply.

"Enough it's drawing some strange creatures who are stealing the Lycan-born only. Why?"

"Why does it matter? The only thing we need is to find whatever den those fuckers come from and destroy it." Gunner punched a fist into his palm.

Quinn couldn't help but ask, "Why didn't you ask the Cabal for help once you realized you had a problem?"

"The committee voted against it. They said inviting them in would be flouting the fact we eschewed their rules." Gunner didn't sound as if he entirely agreed.

"Come on, they have to know the Cabal is already watching." Quinn couldn't hide his incredulity.

"No, they're not. We have a truce."

Erryn snorted in the face of Gunner's apparent naivety. "Do you really think they've been ignoring this town this entire time?"

"We're independent—"

"You're fooling yourself," she harshly interrupted. "They've allowed you to exist because they're curious."

Gunner's lips flattened. "Is that why they sent you?"

"The Cabal approved this mission. However, at the time, they didn't realize I'd be coming to this place. Once I announced my intentions, someone tried to stop me."

"You'd accuse my people and yet it sounds like it's the Cabal who has traitors," Gunner hissed.

Erryn rolled her eyes. "Would you control your

contrived anger? You hate them, I get it. You've decided to label them the big bad because it makes you feel better. Awesome. But they are not the issue at hand. Your monster problem and the fact they keep waltzing in and out abducting people is."

"She's right," Quinn added. "We should be concentrating on the creatures if you want to prevent this from happening in the future."

"I don't think they'll be a problem anymore." A sour statement by Gunner.

"What makes you say that?" Erryn questioned.

"Because Kianna, the girl who was attacked last night, is the last Lycan-born. And her parents are leaving with her today."

"So there are no more Lycan-born females left?" she asked.

"No Lycan-born at all," Gunner asserted.

"You mentioned only females have been abducted. What of the males?"

"There are none."

Erryn blinked. "What? Why not?"

"Because those pregnancies are unpredictable for starters. Even if very careful, and the mother takes certain supplements without fail, the males are volatile in the womb."

"Surely some made it to term?" Erryn queried. She had to be wondering if Ulric's son was the only successful birth of a male.

"A few did. Before the age of five, they were gone."

"They died?" she squeaked.

149

"No, they left. Ran away to never be found."

Could they have survived, perhaps to become the threat that faced them now?

"Small children don't flee." Erryn sounded disturbed by the claim.

"Wolves do." Gunner's grim pronouncement.

"The male children shifted at such a young age?"

"Supposedly. It happened before my arrival here," Gunner explained, shoving his hands in his pockets. "Anyhow, we've not seen many boys come to term. More than a few have been lost in the last trimester."

"And the mothers?"

"Mostly survived. I only know of one since I've arrived that actually died."

"So there's a high miscarriage rate?"

"I wouldn't know. I'm not a numbers guy. You'd have to ask Sascha."

"The doctor for the clinic?"

"Yes." Gunner nodded, leading them down a side street.

A thoughtful-looking Erryn chewed on her thumb as she followed. She obviously brimmed with questions. Hell, so did Quinn. It didn't help the more they learned, the less everything made sense.

Why would monsters go after the Lycan-born? Was it their scent? The very thought had Quinn almost stumbling. What had Erryn said last night? *The Lycan find me irresistible.* The monster went after Erryn.

Could she be... No, surely, she'd have said something. Then again, why would she? It would explain her interest in the babies though. Could it be Dr. Silver was Lycan-born and wondering how that happened? He couldn't exactly ask her in front of Gunner. He glanced at her, but she stared straight ahead.

Probably worried about Ulric's baby. Fuck, he was worried now.

Gunner headed for the church across the street attached to a medical clinic. The sign said "Open" in several languages, and yet the waiting room gaped empty as they entered. The astringent scent of cleanser bothered his nose.

No one sat behind the desk to greet them and ask their business, but Gunner didn't seem bothered.

"Sascha must be making a house call. He runs this clinic with his sister, Joella's help."

"The same one as on the council?"

Gunner nodded.

"You leave the clinic unlocked and unattended?" Erryn tried to not gasp in shock.

"Used to be we left all the doors and windows unlocked before the monster attacks."

"But what of the drugs? Theft?" Even in her lab, paid for by the Cabal, she had to keep everything under lock and key.

"Doesn't happen, and if it did, the punishment would be swift and severe to serve as an example," Gunner announced with a grim expression.

"Where are the bodies?" Quinn asked.

"In the basement."

"I wouldn't have thought your town big enough for a morgue." Erryn noted the single exam room seemed to double as an operating theatre, currently empty, the door wide open as they passed.

"Not a morgue, just a walk-in cold storage area that we use in the winter when the ground is too hard to dig. This way." Gunner led them to a door that opened onto stairs, the tread of them comprised of stone, like the walls.

They descended a good ten feet into a much colder space. The basement suffered from that universal dankness. The lights were single bulbs hung from the ceiling with dangling chains to activate them. Boxes of supplies perched precariously on metal shelving units, but Erryn headed for the door at the far end. Quinn hastened to keep up as she wrenched open the door and peered inside.

"Is this a joke?" she snapped, turning on Gunner.

"What do you mean?" he asked with a frown as he neared enough to peek over her shoulder. "You've got to be fucking kidding me. Motherfuckers!"

The cold storage room was empty. As in no bodies and an even stronger smell of bleach.

"Maybe someone took them elsewhere for examination?" Quinn offered, not able to hide his doubtful tone.

"No one would have moved the three bodies without telling me!" Gunner yelled. "What the fuck!"

He went bolting upstairs while Erryn entered the storage room and crouched, intent on the floor.

"What is it?" Quinn asked, noticing her interest.

"Someone scrubbed this room." The scent of cleanser overwhelmed.

"Why?"

She glanced at him over her shoulder. "Not only did someone not want us examining the bodies, they wanted to make sure we couldn't get a blood sample to test."

"Fuck," Quinn exhaled. Only to snap his fingers. "Joke's on them. We've got tons of DNA samples back at Velma's."

"She washed the floor, remember?"

"But your nightgown was soaked in it," he reminded.

Her expression brightened as she rose to her feet. "We have to get back there. Now."

Her sense of urgency had him almost leaving her behind as he raced back to the nice lady who'd given them shelter. Gunner joined them, expression grim.

Turned out they were too late. Velma stood in the yard, watching over a burning barrel. It took Gunner only a moment to discover Velma had burned the bloodied clothes, leaving them with no bodies, no samples to test, nothing but a certainty that something fucked was going on.

Even Gunner couldn't deny it anymore as he muttered, "Fuck me, we've got a traitor."

12

THE MISSING BODIES rocked Erryn to her core because once she added in the other events—the attacks both by people and monsters, the missing women, the successful births, the Cabal secrets—it became too much to process. Not to mention, nothing made sense.

Which was why she needed to talk to her mentor.

How could the Cabal, even if it was just one member, have hidden Gherdeal from the rest? Even if it were a social experiment—or a test run on pregnancies—it should have been, if not common knowledge, then at least known to all the Cabal members.

But instead, someone had conveniently erased all mention of this town and its inhabitants. Managed to hide the births. The monsters.

As Gunner made some calls and headed back to the clinic, she and Quinn went into Velma's house.

Only they couldn't find any privacy there either, as the roof repair was under way.

Her expression must have shown her agitation because Quinn held tight to her as he led her back out onto the street. They walked hand in hand, but not romantically. Not roughly either. But he strode with determination.

"You might as well ask." She sighed.

"I think I already know the answer, but I'd like to hear it from your lips."

She ducked her head. "By all indications, my father was Lycan."

Despite Quinn expecting the news, his step stuttered.

"And when were you going to tell me?" he growled.

"Never?" she replied honestly.

"Why?" He whirled to face her, expression tight.

"Because it's none of your business."

"It does when it makes you a target!" he practically yelled.

"Usually that's only a problem on full moons. Lycans in their human shape aren't usually bothered by my scent." A scent she'd once more masked with a perfume borrowed from Velma.

"Not a problem?" he huffed. "We're in a town full of Lycans, the full moon is days away, and you didn't think this was important for me to know?"

"I know how to handle it."

"Handle it? You do realize I'm going to shift, right?

And when I do, who's to say I'll be able to control myself around you?"

She shrugged. "I wasn't planning to be around you or anyone else for that matter."

"Kind of hard given we're sharing a bed," he growled.

"I would have claimed a tummy virus and locked myself in the bedroom for the night while you ran and howled and peed on things. By morning, everything would have been fine."

He gaped at her. "You've got to be kidding."

"I don't see why you're so bothered."

"Because...I..." He huffed, his expression wild, angry, and... She couldn't identify the other emotion.

"At least now you understand why the Cabal chose me."

"They know?"

"Not exactly. My mentor, the one who saved me, does. Given my existence, he's the one who convinced the others to let me research Lycans with the eventual goal of studying pregnancies."

He raked a hand through his hair. "Jeezus. Who's your father? Were you raised in a Pack?"

"Never knew him. Mom said he left when I was born."

"But how did she survive the pregnancy? I thought you needed that wolfsbane and stuff."

"I don't know. Maybe it was different because I was female?" She'd long pondered that question and had yet to figure out the answer. Had her mother gotten help?

"How did you find out?"

"Fred, my mentor, was the one who helped me put the pieces together after Joseph's attack."

"Damn."

She shrugged. "And now you know."

"Does anyone else?"

"Other than my mentor, no. And I'd like to keep it that way."

"I'll keep your secret. I'd never do anything to jeopardize you." He reached out to cup her face.

Her chin tilted. "Even if the Cabal orders you to eliminate me?" Because she'd been wondering since the attacks started whether or not they were targeted because her secret had emerged.

"Fuck the Cabal," he growled. Not the sexiest thing to say and yet the most toe tingling because he dipped his head and kissed her.

Kissed her like a man starving and overcome with passion. She wound her arms around his neck and returned the embrace, a tiny part of her warning this was dangerous. Being close to him, a Lycan, could have such a bad consequence.

Yet she couldn't help herself.

A distant shout and a laughed reply interrupted the moment, and they broke the kiss, staring at each other.

"Think they're done fixing the roof?" he asked with a crooked grin.

"Velma would smack us if we tried." His lips turned down in disappointment at her reminder. Only to lift again when she added, "Remember that abandoned barn just outside town?"

They couldn't walk there quickly enough. Holding hands, casting each other glances. Then looking away. Her cheeks heated. She'd not been this eager in forever. Her lovers had been few and far between.

And never a Lycan after the Joseph incident.

Was this even a good idea?

Before she could talk herself out of it, they'd reached the barn. Its door was ajar, inside gloomy with streaks of sunlight breaking through the cracks. They didn't have a bed, but there were some fresh bales of hay stacked within. So not completely abandoned.

Here was to hoping no one interrupted because once their lips locked, Quinn having swung her into his arms, there was no turning back.

Nor did she want to stop.

His touch ignited her. Her blood boiled. Need filled her and demanded release.

When they collapsed on a bale of hay, she uttered a squeak that he caught with a chuckle even as he continued to kiss her.

Their hands tangled as they each sought to strip the other, their shirts getting pulled off and used to buffer the rough straw under their bodies. Pants and shoes hit the ground until they were both naked. Flesh to flesh.

Kissing.

Touching.

She couldn't help but touch him all over, stroking the smooth and strong lines of his back. Digging her nails into his taut ass. He had his thigh between her legs, pressing against her. A hand cupped her breast, the thumb stroking the peak of her nipple.

What she didn't expect was for him to position himself between her legs so that he could taste her.

He buried his face against her sex, his tongue lithely licking and teasing the nub of her clit. He drew sharp cries and had her panting with pleasure. When he flicked her sensitive button with his tongue while fingering her, she came embarrassingly quick.

But he wasn't done. He kept teasing her flesh, and her orgasm stretched, tightening her body, readying her for when he positioned himself over her, the tip of his cock pressing.

She opened her eyes to behold him, expression taut, his eyes blazing with passion. His low growled, "Do you want me to stop?" was the inanest question given the need coursing inside her body.

"Don't you dare stop now," was her grumbled reply as she dragged him down for a kiss, tasting herself on his lips. She sighed into his mouth as he slid into her, hard and long, thick enough to stretch.

They fit together perfectly. They moved together in a rhythm that only made everything feel better. He thrust, and she rolled her hips to take him deep, the tip of him hitting her sweet spot inside, making her gasp. Her pleasure coiled.

Her need demanded more, and so she dug her nails into his back and growled, "Harder."

He groaned as he complied, his pace quickening, his strokes making her keen with the ecstasy of it.

She couldn't have said who came first. She clenched, and it rolled through her, a wave of bliss so intense she forgot to breathe. Her fingers held him almost as tight as her sex.

He panted, and his body went rigid as he found his release.

Together they recovered, flesh to flesh, his cock buried in her sheath, their heart rates taking time to calm.

Nothing bad happened. He didn't suddenly go wild and try to eat her face. On the contrary, he appeared more relaxed than she'd ever seen him.

Until she nibbled his lower lip and said, "I'm not ready to go back yet." She wiggled her hips to let him know what she actually wanted.

He gave it to her again, and the orgasm proved just as intense the second time.

Given hunger began to stir in her belly, it was with great reluctance that they rose to dress themselves. The moment quiet, as if they both feared speaking.

He plucked hay from her hair. She tried not to wince at the marks she'd left on his flesh.

When they were ready to go, he dragged her close for a kiss. A short one.

His thumb rubbed her lower lip. "This wasn't supposed to happen."

And he'd ruined the moment.

"You're right. This is a bad idea." She went to move past him, but he grabbed her arm and spun her back to face him.

"Never said that. I just didn't expect—"

"Listen. I don't know what you think this was." She waved a hand. "But before you get any crazy ideas, I'm not looking for anything that rhymes with relationship. This was just sex."

"Just sex," he repeated, his expression showing no emotion.

"Would you feel better if I said good sex?"

"No!" The word bit out of his clenched jaw.

"Sorry you didn't enjoy it as much as I did." She wasn't about to lie about that. "Next time I need release, I'll ask someone else." She fled him even as he bellowed, "There will be no one else."

He followed her outside with a glare.

"You don't get to decide who I fuck," was her crude reply.

"That was more than fucking, and you know it," he accused.

The very thought terrified. "Don't you dare make this into something it isn't."

"You want me to pretend I'm not obsessed with you? To lie about the fact I think about you all the fucking time?"

"Sounds like a problem for a shrink. Or maybe you need to get laid more often. Whatever the case, you

161

and me?" She drew a circle in the air. "We're partners on a mission. Who fucked. Nothing more."

He would have argued, she could see it in his blazing eyes, only reality intruded.

"Quinn!" Gunner yelled from up the street. "Fucker, I've been looking for you. Good thing someone told me they saw you walking up this way."

Putting on his business face, Quinn turned to his approaching friend. "What's up?"

"A group of us are going out to track the missing child. You in?"

He glanced at her, and she knew his answer. The wrong one. She replied in his stead. "Of course he'll help. Once he sticks me somewhere monster-proof, right?" She cast him a glance.

His jaw tightened. "I am not leaving you undefended."

"It's daytime, and I'm sure we can find a public place with lots of people to keep me company."

Gunner nodded. "Everyone's going to the rec hall attached to the church. Given most of the guys will be in the hunting parties, it's easier to protect just in case."

"Most? Who's staying behind?" Quinn questioned.

"Some of the older men folk, plus some of our sharpest shooters. A few of the women took up target practice when the attacks started. Most of them can shoot as good or better than you and me," Gunner stated with pride.

She could have stuck a pin in it by asking how that

helped in the previous abductions, but she let him have it.

"I am not leaving you alone, Doc."

"Ignore Quinn. He's just a worry wolf." She didn't look at him as she said it. "I'll be fine. Especially if you loan me a cell phone. I'd like to make some calls. Oh, and a laptop with internet access."

"Anything else?" Gunner drawled.

She arched a brow. "As a matter of fact, yes. The medical files of those who got pregnant with Lycan babies. The files for the babies themselves. And any documentation on the previous monster attacks."

"We don't keep those kinds of records for obvious reasons. But," Gunner added, "I can point out at least two mothers when we get to the church, and a bonus for you, they speak English."

"That will do," she accepted graciously.

More so than Quinn, who barked, "I don't like it, Doc. You and I both know you're in danger."

"Then all the more reason for you to put your nose to the ground and sniff out the den of these monsters. Which I'm pretty sure isn't in the church."

His mighty scowl didn't deter her smile.

But it did increase her sass, meaning she added a tart, "Put that testosterone to use, would you, and find that child."

"Only if you promise you won't leave that church!" He stabbed his finger in the direction of the building, now in sight.

"I promise." She rolled her eyes.

163

She had to promise again once inside the holy temple as he dragged her close to mutter, "Don't do anything stupid."

"How can I get in trouble surrounded by women and children?" She grimaced as she glanced over her shoulder where the pews had been pushed against the walls to make room for the children to play. Not many and, if Gunner spoke truly, all human.

"I'm more worried about trouble finding you." He sighed. "When I come back, we need to talk about what happened in the barn."

"I'd rather just repeat it in a bed," she conceded but hastily appended it with, "No strings attached."

"We'll see about this." His ominous reply as he left.

She watched. After all, he had a nice ass.

Would being his partner romantically be that bad? So far, he didn't seem to be suffering any ill effects from their proximity. She'd reserve a decision until after the full moon.

True to his word, Gunner did provide her with a cell phone and a laptop, both of them modern enough she could make an encrypted call to Fred—that went right to voicemail. She kept it brief. *"There is some weird stuff happening in Gherdeal. You might want to send a team."* The laptop required her to download a few items to secure it before she logged onto the Cabal network.

Once in there, she typed up her notes of what she'd encountered thus far. Just in case. If something happened to her, then at least Fred would have a place to start.

The morning passed uneventfully. She paused for lunch because Velma insisted, dragging her to the clinic next door, where a buffet table had been set up. She finally met Joella, the doctor's sister, a woman much flashier than the others she'd met thus far in town. They didn't speak long, mostly because Erryn found her off-putting.

Somehow the afternoon got rowdier, making the interviews she wanted to conduct difficult. Until she remembered the basement in the clinic.

Her first interviewee was Magda. Currently twenty-five years old, she'd aborted in the last trimester.

They sat across from each other in the dank cellar on fold-up chairs she'd scrounged and carried down herself. They'd already gone through the niceties. How old was she when she conceived? Who was the father? What symptoms did she have? Did she recall the treatment?

The hard questions came after that. "You aborted late in your pregnancy. Why?"

"Because it was a boy." A low admission.

She'd heard of people selecting the sex of her baby, but this was her first time encountering someone who did something about it. "Did you not have an ultrasound earlier in your gestation?" she asked because that late in the pregnancy the child was fully formed and often viable, making it traumatic for the mother.

"They couldn't tell for sure. But they suspected, given I needed a strong dose of medication to keep it from kicking the hell out of me. Sorry. I didn't mean to swear." Magda actually covered her mouth with her hand.

"I've said worse. Who performed the procedure to extract the child?"

"Sascha. Our doctor. He put me to sleep, and when I woke, it was done."

"Could I get your permission to excavate the body for study?" Erryn felt awful for asking, but science required it. She could learn a lot from a body, even one in the ground for a while. At the very least, DNA would still be intact.

"There was no body. The doctor got rid of it so I wouldn't have to deal with the trauma."

Which led to her wondering how the doctor removed the fetus. At that stage, the child would be too large to simply vacuum. "Did he give you a C-section?"

Magda shook her head. "It came out the normal way. I was sore for weeks."

Meaning a vaginal delivery. It chilled Erryn to think the doctor then snuffed the life of that wee baby. So what if it were Lycan from birth. It blew her mind to think people would rather kill than try and find a way to help these children. If he was indeed killing them.

"Did you see the fetus before burial?" she asked.

Magda's lips turned down. "No. I couldn't bear to, and the doctor didn't recommend it."

Meaning it was possible the doctor kept the baby, and if he had, then he might have a way to keep them from going feral. She hoped so because Michael, the baby she'd helped come to fruition, might stand a chance. She'd hate for him to be doomed like the other Lycan born children. The pain it would cause...

I won't allow that to happen.

Once Magda left, she talked to Brianna, who had a slightly different story. She was pregnant with twins. Only the girl survived. Apparently, the boy—the runt of the two—died within minutes of birth. Brianna never even got to hold him.

And the body of the child? Also disposed of by the doctor. A doctor she really wanted to chat with.

After Brianna left, Erryn remained in the basement, enjoying the solitude for work even as she grumbled at the lack of signal. Once she finished typing up her notes, she'd head upstairs and see what they had laid out for dinner because, according to her stomach, it neared.

Scratch.

A noise from a far corner drew her attention.

She rose and angled her head to look. Probably a rodent. She packed up her things and was prepared to head upstairs when a draft blew past her cheek.

Odd.

As she strode past a shelving unit for the stairs, she never even saw them.

Nor could she avoid the burlap sack yanked over her head.

13

AN UNEASY QUINN kept looking back over his shoulder. Leaving Erryn bothered the fuck out of him, but at the same time, he could only argue so much.

She'd raised valid points. It was daytime, and she was surrounded by people and certainly capable of looking after herself. On the other hand, fucked-up monsters looking for Lycan-born females were on the loose.

But that wasn't even the most disturbing thing. What did she mean it was just sex? Would she really deny the insane attraction between them? The bodily connection that went beyond good fucking sex?

He finally got what his buddies talked about. Finally succumbed. Found his one.

And she had no interest in him as a mate.

"Hey, I realize you're still horny, but I need you focused on the here and now." Gunner snapped his fingers.

Quinn shot him a glare. "I'm worried."

"She'll be fine. We've never had an attack in the daytime."

He and Gunner had chosen to split off as a pair and, rather than hunt from the last location of the missing child, started at Velma's house. Because track one and they might find them all. A climb to the roof top hadn't yielded a trail to follow. Overnight rain had washed it clean. Meaning they had little hope of finding it outside the town, and yet they trudged through the tall weeds past the last house, keeping a keen eye open for any possible trace.

"Let's talk possible traitors." Quinn knew Gunner had to be thinking about it. "How did your sniper in the church miss the monsters coming?"

Gunner grunted. "Says he went for a fucking piss. Came back, the action was done."

"Convenient timing."

"I would have said bad luck. And before you even say it, I trust Smith. He lost his daughter a few years ago, which led to his wife committing suicide. He's been dying to get vengeance."

"How do these creatures know where to find the girls?"

"It's got to be a scent thing." The most obvious answer that Gunner provided.

"But you're talking about people inside houses in some cases. Tracking is all well and good, but these seem awfully targeted."

"I know." A soft reply. A heavy sigh eased from

Gunner as he trudged through foliage, crushing it without care. "I really don't want to believe it. This town, this way of living... It gave me such hope that one day Lycan and human could live together. The thought that someone, one of us," he corrected, his voice raspy, "would help these fucking mutants steal our children... I can't..."

"And yet it would explain a lot."

Gunner whirled on him. "Except you and your woman are wrong. Those monsters aren't the people of this village."

"Did you happen to notice the tattoo on the one that first attacked us? On the arm, bicep.

Gunner frowned as he resumed walking. "I didn't see it. I never actually inspected the bodies. Just dumped them in the cold room to deal with in the morning."

"I couldn't see all of it, given a clump of hair obscured part of it, but it looked like a circle crossed with—"

"A dagger. The circle represented the full moon." Gunner spoke softly.

"So you did see it?"

"Not on the beast. But there used to be a guy a couple of years ago. A loner. He came into Gherdeal thinking he could be a shit. Name of Orville. He had a tattoo like you described, right here." He pointed to his arm.

"I'm going to assume on the full moon he turned into a regular wolf and not the beast man we saw?"

"Yeah, he was wolf, and not particularly strong either unless he was harassing those weaker than him. We ran him out of town for trying to force himself on one of the women."

"I'm surprised you didn't kill him."

"I would have if I'd caught him," Gunner grumbled. "Someone must have given him the heads-up we were coming for him, because the coward fled."

"And returned changed," Quinn mused loud. "Erryn's gonna want to know about that."

"Why?"

"Because something obviously happened to this Orville after he left. And whatever it was changed him on a molecular level."

"You think someone experimented on him?" Gunner sounded incredulous.

"Don't sound so surprised. After all, look at how we came about." A sobering reminder.

They walked for hours, back and forth along the edge of the forest and a slight distance within, looking for tracks, a scent, a tuft of hair, anything.

Late morning, a far-off yodel drew their attention. Without talking, they both took off at a run, heading deep into the forest, the thick branches overhead still full of leaves despite the fall weather blocking most of the sun. By the time they reached the man who'd yelled, a few of them had gathered and stood over a single print in the mud on the shore of a stream.

Bare foot, clawed, a few strands of hair left behind.

"We fucking found one!" Gunner exclaimed in

surprise. Immediately he barked out orders. "Jenson and Wallace, follow the shore upstream. Opi and Sutton, down. Herman, Dill, Quinn, and I will cross and see if we can pick up anything on the other side."

The stream wasn't deep, but it sure ran cold. Quinn grimaced. He knew he was getting old, given how much he wanted to soak his feet somewhere warm, maybe snuggled under a blanket with a certain doctor.

The muddy far bank held no tracks, but that didn't daunt the searchers. They split, Gunner and Quinn following the shore of the stream north. The beast had most likely waded in the water to hide its scent and could have emerged anywhere.

They found it almost a mile away. A perfect pawed footprint in the mud. Too perfect. It seemed too easy. Gunner had claimed they couldn't track the monster, and yet here they were, the trail obvious to even the most unsavvy.

But did his friend pause to wonder why?

Nope. His excitement grew as he found traces here and there. Hair caught on branches. A claw print in soft soil.

The last clue ended on the edge of a cliff. The ravine stretched far below, the river slicing through it violent with rapids. The rocky face sheer with few handholds.

"Do you think it jumped?" Gunner asked, eyeing the other side.

"If it did, no way it made it across." They glanced down. "No way it survived if it fell either."

"Why would it kill itself?" Gunner huffed in agitation. "Do you think it had Steffi when it did?" Steffi being the stolen child.

"I think we got played."

"What's that supposed to mean?"

"This convenient trail to the edge of this cliff." Quinn waved a hand. "It wants us to think it died so we stop looking."

"As if that will happen," Gunner growled. He flattened himself and appeared to be contemplating a suicidal climb.

"Don't be a fucking moron. You'll kill yourself if you try to follow it down there."

"I have to find it."

"Hard to do if you're dead."

"What do you suggest then?" an angry Gunner asked.

"I suggest we get some rope. Picks if you've got them. Does anyone in town rock climb at all?"

"No, but Jenson has an ATV with a winch."

"Then what are we waiting for?"

Given Gunner's worry they'd miss something if they all went back, two men were left to watch over the cliff in case the monster had fooled them and remained close by. The rest headed back for town, discouraged by their failure.

The last of the afternoon sun waned as they

emerged from the forest well before dark, and yet he hastened his step as a bad feeling hit him in the gut.

Gunner's murmured, "I'm sure she's fine," didn't help.

The houses mostly remained dark with only the church providing a bright beacon against encroaching darkness. As he entered, his gaze went to the milling people, mostly women, some cradling children. Human ones according to Gunner. Many of the men in the town had chosen to sire them before getting the change. He didn't see Erryn among them. But he did spot Velma.

It took some miming before she understood his request.

"Doctor. Down." She pointed to her left and a door that led to the clinic. Inside, he found more folks and tables being loaded with food for dinner. No Erryn but Velma had said down.

It didn't surprise him Doc had chosen a quiet spot like the basement. She wasn't big on socializing.

He went down the stairs, smelling that awful fragrance she'd borrowed from Velma.

"Doc?" he called but didn't get a reply.

He didn't panic until he'd gone around the basement twice and not found her. Her terrible perfume lingered, but she was gone.

At least from the basement. Maybe she'd needed to use a bathroom. He headed back upstairs and did a frantic search of all the spaces, which caught Gunner's eye.

"What's wrong?"

"I can't find Erryn."

Gunner's brows rose, but he didn't question, rather turned to Velma and spoke to her rapid-fire.

"You looked in the clinic basement?" Gunner asked.

"Yeah, she's not there."

She wasn't to be found anywhere.

He'd failed to protect Erryn.

And to make matters worse? When he returned to the basement, he encountered a ghost.

14

BEING KIDNAPPED SUCKED. Being kidnapped and having her head covered in burlap, tossed over a hairy shoulder, and carted off like a sack of potatoes? Even worse, but most terrifying of all? Knowing Gunner and the others had never managed to track any of the beasts, meaning Erryn was on her own for rescue.

A good thing she wasn't easily daunted. Rather than panic and give in to hysterics, she began to note what she could. For one, her abductor didn't climb any stairs. It could only mean the basement had a hidden entrance—or in this case exit. Not surprising given the age of the place. Most likely how they'd removed the beast bodies the previous night without being noticed.

While she couldn't be entirely sure, they appeared to be moving in a tight space. The echoes of sound, the drips of water, and even the occasional rumble overhead indicated a tunnel of some kind under the town.

A subterranean route linking who knew how many houses, a realization that led to her lightbulb moment.

That's how the creatures have been getting in and out without being found. Gunner and his crew assumed the creatures were infiltrating and scattering to the woods and mountains beyond the town. They never even suspected they might be popping up from underground burrows, and surely if anyone knew of these secret passages, they would have been searching and exploring them. Quinn and the others would never find her.

But in better news, she wasn't entirely without resource. The kidnappers would assume her weak. They'd be in for a surprise. Given she faced unknown odds, she'd have to time her escape just right.

They didn't travel too long or too far, even taking into account the monster's loping run. The creature paused abruptly, and she heard a thud, pause, then two hard knocks as it pounded on something.

A series of unidentifiable noises followed that culminated in the creak of a door opening. The pure darkness she'd endured suddenly became filtered light through the tight woven canvas.

They'd arrived. The question being, where?

An unknown voice spoke, the words raspy. "Put her in cell three. It should be ready."

She didn't know what surprised more, that she was being imprisoned or the fact the monster took orders. It actually made perverse sense. How else did they know exactly where to strike and who to take?

177

But why were they taking people? That was the real question.

She had no way to brace herself as she was dumped without ceremony onto a hard floor. She grunted and rolled, her arms caught in the sack but not for long. With the beast not holding her tight, she could wiggle out and get to a sitting position that showed her in an honest-to-god dungeon.

Stone walls. No window. Not even a set of bars she could cling to and scream hopelessly. Deeper than it was wide, she doubted she could lie straight across. Good thing she kind of wanted to curl up in a fetal position.

As she swiveled her head, she glimpsed a hole in the floor, and she didn't need to be told that was her toilet. While it didn't emit a foul stench, she knew enough about history to recognize its use.

No bed. Not even a blanket. Just the faint scent of bleach permeating the air. Judging by the light spots in the stone, they'd recently scrubbed some stains. Stains she'd prefer not to think about.

The door to the cell, a thick wooden thing banded in metal, remained open, and seeing a chance, she pushed to her feet and almost made it to the frame when a man blocked her escape. She paused to take him in. He wore dark gray cargo pants with many pockets. A belt cinched tight around his slim build. His plaid shirt was tucked in. To complete the outfit, dusty steel-toed boots. His hair color must have been either very blond or close to white, hard to tell given he'd shorn it to the scalp. She leaned to the latter given the lines marking his face. The scar bisecting his features from his jaw across his cheek and ending high on his forehead appeared old, given it had the white-gray ridged appearance that came with age.

Most important, she didn't recognize him at all.

The stranger saw her staring, and his lips twisted. "At last, we meet."

"Who are you?" she asked.

"The village folk call me Sascha."

"The doctor?" she exclaimed.

"You sound surprised. I had intended to meet with you sooner, but my work was keeping me busy."

"What work? The clinic was empty." Talking to the folk during lunch she'd gotten the impression it wasn't used much. Lycans being pretty healthy to start with meant the humans they lived with didn't deal with as many of the viruses rampant in the more populated areas. Mostly he handled broken limbs, stitches, and babies. According to Magda, given Sascha's less-than-busy schedule, he volunteered his time doing remote wellness checks to those who couldn't make it to see him in the village. Sounded like an awesome doctor, or she'd thought at the time. She now saw it for a perfect excuse.

"I see by your expression you've figured it out. The clinic is but a cover to give me access to the villagers."

The mention of access slewed her gaze to the beast standing just past him. "You're working with those—those—" What to call them? Wolfmen sounded juvenile, but "creatures" no longer seemed apt. They took orders and accomplished sophisticated kidnappings, meaning they had some kind of intelligence.

"I believe you are referring to the Lycan-Z? It's what I call them since they are the next generation."

"Generation of what?" she blurted out.

"Lycan evolution."

She couldn't help but laugh. "You call that advanced?"

The insult pinched his features. "I'm still working on perfecting the technique."

"You're experimenting on people," she pointed out.

"Not any that will be missed."

"That's a terrible thing to say." Some lines shouldn't ever be crossed or justified. Not even for science. Although she'd come close. She'd taken a chance with Honey and the baby. A risk that could have backfired had she not gotten access to some recipes from an old book owned by the alpha of the Toronto Pack. Apparently, Lycan ancestors had employed some remedies to treat some conditions. Like pregnancy.

"I see no problem with culling a few," the doctor bragged. "The world has too many people. The media and its climate warriors keep shouting it at us. I am doing everyone a favor. Not only am I making something of the undesirables, I'm also ensuring they won't engender new useless carbon emitters."

She almost gagged at the sourness left in her mouth once he finished. "You're sick."

"No, I am evolving. Not exactly where I need to be yet. But soon. And this time I won't have to rely on the gamble of an archaic bite."

"You're not Lycan." It hit her with surprise.

"I was supposed to be," he railed. "I was chosen and much more fit than many. But my body rejected it, no matter how many times I got the bite."

"Is this your revenge then? Working in a village catering to Lycans so you can murder their children?" The evil just about stole her breath.

"Science appreciates their sacrifice."

The depravity hit her hard. He really had no remorse for what he'd done. "So you've killed them?"

"Not all. The most recent ones are still alive and helping to further my studies. You see, I started out studying the bite itself and what about it caused the Lycan change. It wasn't easy finding an alpha I could use. I kept having to move my lab around. The longest one before this lasted almost two years and was subsidized by the military. Years more before I managed to home in on the mutation passed in the saliva to the host. A mutation that is broken in the bitten."

She couldn't help but be curious and ask, "What mutation?"

"As if you don't know. I've read your studies. You've already found it."

He confirmed they talked about the same marker. "I don't understand why you call it broken though."

"Because in Lycan-born females it's perfect and complete."

"How can it be perfect when they can't shift?" she replied, even as her heart thudded.

"I'll admit it's odd they can't, and yet there's no denying what they can do. No wonder the Cabal banned their births."

"The Cabal banned pregnancies because it's dangerous to the mothers and the fetus."

"What isn't dangerous? So what if a few birthing bitches died? It is a fact of life that death is always nearby." Sasha leaned in the doorway, blocking her only escape. Even if she got past him, she had the Lycan-Z to contend with. How many? she wondered.

"You encouraged the pregnancies in the village. You put all those women at risk."

"Bah, more survived than died, and a few even had more than one live birth. The pregnancies are more viable than the Cabal lets on."

"Lycan pregnancies require specialized care."

Sascha's lips stretched into a smirk. "I'm aware. Who do you think has been helping the mothers of the village successfully come to term?"

"You helped them so you could steal their children for your sick experiments." Experiments that led to wolfmen who took sadistic orders.

"You say that with disdain. Wait until you grasp what I've accomplished."

"I already have. It's standing right behind you."

"The Lycan-Z were an early protype. I've been working on different models. Would you like to see?"

Not really, since he sounded insane, but at the

same time, she needed to know more. How else would she escape?

"Fine, show me."

"Ah, so there is a scientist hidden inside there after all. You see, you and I aren't so different after all."

Yes, they were. And he'd die for even suggesting otherwise.

He shifted out of the door to her cell, and she hesitated only a second before emerging into the dungeon proper. "Where are we?" she asked, noting the octagonal space with its tilted floors leading to a large grate in the middle. Eight doors. The thick wood reinforced with metal bands had no markings, yet she knew one of them led to a tunnel. They had wooden bars set in brackets across them. Old school.

"We are in a castle abandoned a few centuries ago. Most of its upper levels have collapsed, but with a little bit of work, we've managed to convert the main floor into a lab."

"Why put your lab in a remote spot? Why not use the clinic?" she asked, hoping her interest hid how she studied everything she saw—only two Lycan-Z and definite sobbing behind a door.

He cast her a grin. "Silly question, Doctor Silver. The villagers are too simple-minded to grasp what I'm doing. They would get emotional and violent. Best I keep them in the dark."

"How long have you been using the tunnel into the village?"

"Not long after I set up shop. Once I found it, I

quickly realized its use. This entire time I've been working under their noses. Studying the Lycan mystery. Do you know there was a time I did it with the Cabal's approval? But then some of them got squeamish. One of them even tried to stop me." He fingered his scar.

"What did you do to earn their displeasure?" she asked, even as she suspected the answer.

"Initially, I sought to understand how lycanthropy worked and if it could only be passed along via an unpredictable bite. After all, it was just saliva introduced into the bloodstream. What if I injected it instead? Alas, that avenue of research failed. A few of my test subjects died. Others had to be put down."

"People aren't animals," she huffed.

He waved a hand. "Again, might I remind you I wasn't using anybody that would be missed, but the narrow-sighted on the Cabal didn't see it as advancing their cause. They tried to have me killed. Lucky for me, I proved stronger."

"You switched from a roving lab to set up shop in Romania. Why?" she questioned.

"Because I tired of making progress, only to have to flee suddenly. It helped I made a friend who helped me stay under the radar. They pointed me in the direction of Gherdeal. Not only is out it of the way with plenty of subjects to play with, but I was welcomed with open arms. You should have seen their delight at having a doctor friendly to the Lycan cause."

"You're not Lycan," she reminded.

"Not for lack of trying." His expression twisted as he led her through a door that seemed like the others but for the stairs on the other side. No complicated locks thus far.

They went up stone steps to the main floor of the castle, a place reinforced with four-by-fours, all to accommodate the former great hall full of medical equipment. Beeping and humming machines, metal counters with computers, a few beds, one of them occupied.

A little girl lay asleep, strapped to a medical bed, IVs in both arms.

Erryn rushed to the child's side. "What are you doing to her?"

"Taking what I need." As he spoke, a machine beeped. The IV on the left began drawing blood.

"No. Stop it. She's just a kid." She eyed the IV but hesitated at pulling it out. Then had no chance to do anything since a beast grabbed her in a hold that pinned her arms.

"She won't die. Not yet. The strong ones last months." Sascha's callous reply as the blood kept draining. When it seemed he'd bleed the child dry, the second IV suddenly opened up, filling the child with a replacement.

"You're taking her blood."

"Indeed, I am. Did you know the natural born have special traits? For example, the males start turning at a young age, and they don't need the moon. Every single one has alpha traits. Which explains why the Cabal fears them."

"Those women who miscarried late in their term, that was your doing?" she accused.

His smile confirmed it before his words.

"It occurred to me that a man of my vision, with enemies, needs an army loyal to him alone. The males, when indoctrinated at a young age, suit that purpose."

"What of those boys that disappeared from their homes?"

"Handled before they became a nuisance."

"That's sick."

"Only because you lack vision. Look at you, a Lycan-born female with so much potential, and you wasted it on petty studies."

Her blood went cold. He had no way of knowing the truth of her birth. "I'd rather waste it than be like you."

"And that's the problem. You don't have a killer instinct. You're weak. Like the rest of your sex," he said with a sneer then to the Lycan-Z holding Erryn, "Strap her to the bed. I want a look at her blood."

Her blood ran cold, fear icing her veins. He couldn't see. Mustn't see. Wouldn't...

A heated anger took hold. It grew as she thought of the lives he'd taken, the people he'd hurt, the danger he posed.

"Tell your pet to let me go, or else."

Said pet growled lightly behind her. Hunh. It didn't like that particular insult.

"Or else what?" taunted Sascha, who wasn't a true doctor. A real one would have never caused such harm.

"Do you know the real reason why the Cabal fear the Lycan-born?" She caught his gaze and held it.

"Let me guess, you're going to tell me?" he taunted.

"Actually, I'm more a fan of showing." Before she could twitch a single muscle, a sudden silence filled the place as the power went out.

"Check the generator," Sascha snapped. "Someone get me a light."

He stepped away from Erryn. A mistake.

For him.

15

A SHOCKED QUINN entered the basement, expecting to see Erryn, but instead there was a ghost. A solid one that had him muttering, "Scarecrow?"

Quinn might have thought he hallucinated, only Gunner suddenly joined him and stopped dead. His expression turned ashen, and his jaw dropped as he blinked in surprise. "Is that...?" He couldn't say it and pointed.

It was Scarecrow and wasn't. The man before him didn't have a wild mane of hair and shaggy beard. He appeared neatly trimmed, his body thicker than the guy who'd bitten them in prison. It didn't help he'd dressed very modern in faded jeans and blue flannel layered with a puffy vest. But those eyes and that scent... It might have been sixteen years, but Quinn remembered.

"Hello, boys," the older man said. "Been a while."

"What the fuck? You're supposed to be dead!"

Gunner yelled.

"Not yet, although people have tried." Scarecrow offered a lopsided grin.

For some reason Quinn wanted to run screaming. Something felt very off about the situation. "I don't understand..." Quinn shook his head. "You were practically dead last time we saw you."

"I'll explain once I find Doctor Silver. Do you know where she is?"

Suspicion had him immediately snapping, "How do you know Doc?"

"She works for me. As do you actually."

Quinn's mouth rounded. The more the man spoke, the more the voice sounded familiar. It should be since he'd been his main point of contact for years. "You're Rick. Cabal Rick."

"In the flesh."

Quinn's lips pursed. "All this time... Did you know who I was? Did you even remember me?" He quickly corrected to, "Us?"

"It's not like we exchanged names, and I was kind of fucked up at the time." Rick shrugged. "Looks like you boys made out fine."

"If by fine you mean stumbling onto a pack."

"A fine one," Rick added with a nod.

Gunner shoved himself into Rick's face. "You know what I find odd is that you've been alive all this time and yet this is the first time we've run into each other."

"Because you run into other pack members so

often. Let me ask, have you ever met Quinn's friends?"

"You didn't even try to find us." Gunner's accusation was almost plaintive.

"Didn't I?" Rick eyed Quinn. "Or did you think Griffin found you by accident that night?" He swiveled his gaze to Gunner. "You, on the other hand, kept rejecting every helping hand sent your way."

"I don't need your help," Gunner sneered. "And what of Brock? Or are you going to tell me you made him the bloodbag for some vamps?"

"What of him? He's too alpha for a pack, and not interested in leading one, but you know what he's good at? Dealing with Lord Augustus and his court."

"I can't believe you never reached out," Quinn softly accused. "We had nightmares about leaving you."

The admission turned the corners of Rick's lips down. "For that I am truly sorry. We knew each other such a short time. And most of it, I was delirious with malnutrition."

"What happened to you? How did you end up there?" Quinn asked. He'd never been able to put a name to Scarecrow's face.

"I was tricked by someone I knew and captured. It was a very bad time for me. Luckily, we found each other and escaped."

"And the sicko who tortured you?" Gunner asked.

"I killed him." A grim admission. "Now, can we go find Ryn?"

The nickname Quinn had heard before startled

him, mostly because it suggested familiarity. "Are you the guy who saved Doc when she was attacked in university?"

"That's me, but she saved herself. I just helped her cover it up."

"Wait, she killed the dude who mauled her?" Quinn couldn't help the surprised lilt.

"Yes. Any more questions?"

He had a ton, but most of those replies should come from Doc's lips. "I could have sworn Doc told me she worked for a guy called Fred."

"She does. My real name is Frederick. She's the only one who calls me Fred, as in Fred Flintstone, on account she claims I'm stuck in caveman times."

"Sounds like Doc," Quinn replied with a slight smile.

"Where is she? I've been trying to get in touch, but her cell phone went dead. Or is it this place? I've been failing to get a signal for the last hour."

"We're in a bit of a cell phone dead spot. It only works sporadically," Gunner informed.

As for Quinn, it killed him to admit, "Doc appears to have disappeared. She was last seen in this basement." He swept a hand. "We think the monsters got her."

"Monsters?" Rick repeated. "Tell me more."

"Hold on a second. I want to go back to the part where we thought you were dead! You think you can just be like I tried to manipulate your lives and it's all good," Gunner exclaimed, having gotten over his shock. "It's not okay! You made me into a fucking were-wolf. I lost my fiancée because of it."

"Because you chose to break things off."

"I had no choice," Gunner insisted.

"Wrong," Rick chided. "You could have told her. If your love was true, she would have understood."

"And if not, she'd have died to protect the packs," a bitter rejoinder.

"I didn't make the rules."

"But you are in a position to change them," Gunner retorted.

"I'm trying, but it's not easy. There are seven Cabal members, and new laws require a unanimous vote. It took a bit of charm and quite a few threats to convince them to allow Ryn a chance to even study the idea of pregnancy."

"And yet the Cabal has known it's possible for a while now," Quinn interjected. "You knew about Gherdeal."

"Not in the sense you're implying," Rick defended. "It appears we've been fed false information about the village. Our source claimed all pregnancies failed. So imagine my surprise when Ryn approached me with those DNA results she hacked."

"Meaning you knew the Cabal had a traitor," Quinn huffed, his anger getting hotter.

"Suspected, but one cannot accuse without evidence. The moment I heard the plane blew up, I knew she was in trouble, but Ryn isn't one to back down from trouble."

"I've noticed," he grumbled.

"I tried to reach her, but she wasn't the only one to suffer delays on her trip."

"Sorry to say you're too late. She's gone with the rest of them." Gunner offered a fatalistic reply.

Rick frowned. "I take this has to do with the monsters Quinn mentioned."

"I don't know what else to call them. They're like wolfmen."

"Lycan?"

"No, literally wolfmen. Two legs. Hairy. Claws. But imagine them on hands."

For a moment, Rick looked like he'd seen a ghost. He reeled. "That can't be true."

"You've seen those before."

"Only once. We have to hurry. Ryn is in great danger."

The man didn't head for the stairs but the walls, running his hands over them, nose close as well, scenting the stone. He stopped in a spot and sniffed up and down before glancing at them over his shoulder. "This is how they got in."

"There's a secret room?" It sounded medieval. Quinn glanced around. Okay, so maybe it was possible.

"How do we open it?" Gunner asked.

"There must be some kind of clasp." They kept running their hands over the wall with Quinn moving away from the doorway looking for— "Aha!"

"What did you find?" Rick asked.

"A clean spot." Quinn smelled cleaner on the wall

right on a stone that seemed rather smooth in one spot. He shoved. It didn't make a noise. Neither did the door as it swung open, revealing a tunnel.

Gunner grimaced. "You've got to be shitting me. Has this been here this entire time?"

"Didn't you say the village was practically abandoned when the Lycans started moving in?" Quinn sought to offer some consolation to his friend. "Stands to reason no one remembered a tunnel existed."

It was more than just one, they realized once they found themselves a lantern to guide their path. Not that they needed it. The smell of a wolfman—of something wrong—would have led them the right way despite the junctions. Gunner didn't say much when they passed the shoe of a child. What could anyone say?

Quinn walked behind Rick and couldn't help but murmur, "I'm sorry we left you behind."

"On my orders. Which saved me. I couldn't be found with you. The military would have never let me go given they were responsible for what happened."

He blinked. "What?"

"That prison where we met? It was a testing facility run by the military."

"Testing for what?" he exclaimed.

Scarecrow arched a brow. "Do you really have to ask?"

"Wait, our side caught us? You mean, we weren't real prisoners of war?" Gunner tossed over his shoulder, showing he listened.

"In a sense you were because the military would have disavowed had it been discovered."

"Why didn't the Cabal act?"

"Because they aren't omniscient. We try to prevent these kinds of things, but sometimes evil slips past us."

Quinn's stomach clenched. "The military used us."

"Used us all."

"That can't be true," Gunner argued. "The military discharged us. Why would they if they knew?"

"Because it wasn't a well-known secret. Only a few people on our side were aware of it, and I took care of them once I made it out," Rick announced. "With a little bit of help, the Cabal wiped everything they could to protect Lycans."

"Not well enough. Seems like someone has been playing god again," Gunner grimly announced. "Those wolfmen we told you about have been taking kids and killing folks who get in their way."

"Children?" Rick exhaled.

"Lycan-born ones," Gunner added. "Is the military behind it?"

Rick shook his head. "Not this time. It's worse. I fear it is Lycans who are playing with lives."

"You mean the Cabal," Gunner barked. "Untrustworthy power-mongers."

"Not all of us. But yes, one for sure, and at the same time, there is no way they could have achieved anything unless some of the villagers were helping."

"No way would they be complicit." Gunner still clung to his stubborn version of reality.

"Money talks."

"And what does this have to do with Doc? Why take her?" Quinn asked. "She's not a kid."

"No, she is just the only Lycan-born female who made it to adulthood."

Quinn's jaw dropped. "Seriously?"

"Yes, unfortunately."

"Why unfortunate?" Gunner asked before Quinn could.

"Because it makes Ryn special," Rick added.

"Does this have to do with her scent, and the fact it drives Lycans wild?" Quinn wanted to know more. Had to know. The last thing he wanted was for something he couldn't control to harm Erryn.

"You've noticed."

Quinn shrugged. "She smells nice, but not in an I-want-to-eat-her kind of way."

"That's because only the shifted can perceive her particular scent."

"Which explains the wolfman that came after her last night." Quinn paused then added, "She killed it."

"Of course she did. Ryn is capable of defending herself."

"Yet here you are looking for her," Gunner pointed out as they passed a junction and kept following the scent."

"Because I care about her."

A feeling Quinn understood all too well. "You said before we had to hurry. You know who took her."

"Let's hope I am wrong."

Gunner whispered, "Shh. Door up ahead."

They went silent and extinguished the lantern, doing their best to reach the portal without being noticed. No one stood guard, and the wolfman scent passed on to the other side.

A groping of the solid panel revealed no lock, no handle, and it didn't yield when pushed.

They retreated a distance to confer in low tones.

"I don't suppose either of you has an axe hidden on their person?" Rick asked.

"Too much noise. We don't want to give them warning," Quinn advised.

Rick rubbed his chin. "Since it's barred from the inside, whoever brought Ryn must have a way to signal to gain entry."

"You going to tap out 'Shave and a Haircut' to see what happens?" Quinn retorted.

"The door isn't an option, so why not backtrack a bit and see if we can find another exit? Maybe if we're close enough, we'll be able to come at them from above ground." Gunner provided the most feasible plan of action.

They returned to the last junction and went left first, into a dead end caused by a collapse. To the right, however, they didn't have to go far before they encountered stairs with a very faint hint of wolfman. They emerged into an old mausoleum, the death of its occupants so long ago the scent of it didn't linger.

But that of the wolfmen and cigarettes did.

Once they emerged, they could hear a hum that had Quinn whispering, "Generator."

Not entirely unheard of in the remote parts given electrical lines were costly to run and maintain. As they traversed the overgrown graveyard, they noticed a sliver of light bisecting the darkness.

Without making a verbal decision, they chose not to speak. Hand gestures returned, familiar as the day they memorized them. And Rick appeared to know them as well.

They eased their way to the stone wall of a building partially collapsed and buried in a vines. To the west, a dirt driveway held a large pickup truck. The front doors to the castle had been replaced with thick metal versions guarded by wolfmen.

East, to the back of the castle, the loud hum of the generator prevented the guy having a cigarette from hearing them. He sat in a chair, rifle across his lap, puffing away.

Before they could retreat and plan, Gunner strode forward, drawing the man's gaze. It widened, and his mouth opened. He began chattering fast, but Gunner wasn't having it.

Before the guy could lift his gun to shoot, Gunner dove on him, and there was no real struggle. A fast-moving Gunner snapped his neck and glared at the dropped body. "May you rot in hell for what you did." He spat and turned away.

Quinn didn't ask if he knew the man. Seemed kind of obvious.

The generator drew their attention next. Shutting it off would notify those inside that something was amiss. At the same time, it also provided a fantastic distraction. They would send someone to check it out, allowing them to pick them off in small groups rather than all at once on their turf.

"Ready?" Rick asked. At their nod, rather than smash or yank wires, Rick simply turned the generator off.

The sudden silence didn't last long though, as sharp yips and cries, which turned into screams of pain, erupted from inside.

What the fuck was happening inside?

"Quick. We need to get in there," Ricked declared, leading the way.

"What's happening?" Gunner asked as they trailed Rick, who followed the electrical cords from the generator to the ruins.

The men snaked through an overgrown opening, most likely a window that had long lost its shutters. It took only a bit of clearing before a body could fit through the overgrowth. It dropped them into a storage room with power bars and more electrical cords snaking out of the room.

They kept on Rick's heels as he hurried them through the castle, which smelled much like a hospital. And a morgue. Death existed inside these walls. Blood, too. But the thing that had Quinn almost snarling was a scent he knew. That hideous perfume Erryn had borrowed from Velma.

She was here!

Hopefully alive. The battle raging in the next room had him worried. The last time she had vanquished a wolfman, she'd had a poker and help from Velma. What would they walk into?

As they entered the bigger space, Quinn readied to rush in despite it being too dark to see. Rick threw out an arm to keep him in check, hissing, "Wait, she's not done."

Not done what? He didn't understand. Something fought. One of them lost. The coppery tang of blood filled the air, along with agonized pants.

He wanted to call out to Erryn, but as if reading his mind, Rick murmured, "Shh."

A thud as a body hit the floor had Quinn jerking and shoving past Rick's arm. He couldn't help but yell, "Doc, I'm here. Where are you?"

The room was so fucking dark he couldn't see a hand in front of his face. But he sensed he wasn't alone. The hair on his body lifted. His nose twitched.

He breathed in deep, feeling himself tingle. Knowing where she stood.

He pivoted just as Gunner flanked him and lit their lantern from the tunnel. In the bright light, he caught a glimpse of movement and hair, heard a loud and sharp bark that had him wincing. In that half-second of inattention, the thing in the room leapt for the wall and tore through the hastily erected drywall sheets and through the plywood covering the window.

He didn't immediately follow. He turned around

in the room, looking for Erryn. The faint remnants of that awful perfume were overwhelmed by the blood. So much blood. And body parts. Arm here. Head there.

He closed his eyes to ignore the gore, concentrating on Erryn, waiting for that moment where he would once more detect her location. "Come on, Doc. Where are you?" he muttered aloud.

"Gone, you idiot," Rick muttered. "Who do you think ran off?"

He blinked. "Wait, that was Erryn?"

"That's impossible," Gunner huffed. "She's a woman. They can't shift."

"Her father was an alpha, and she was bitten under the full moon by an alpha," Rick explained as he exited the room and searched for the front door.

Quinn almost tripped at the news and raced after Rick exclaiming, "What the fuck did you just say?"

"No time now. We have to help Ryn. That sick bastard can't be allowed to get his hands on her." Rick found the front doors to the castle open wide. While the moon was bright, it lacked fullness, but it clearly showcased the strange tableaux caught in the cleared area where they'd parked.

A wolfman with long, silky hair with frosted tips, wearing clothes, held up a man by his shirt and snarled.

Actually, that was a wolfwoman. Or would it be wolf doc? Didn't matter. They'd found Erryn, and she was pissed!

16

THE BLOOD LUST took Erryn at the threat on her life, as she'd known it would since she hadn't been taking any wolfsbane to suppress her more feral side. Like an alpha, it took adrenaline to invoke, and she brimmed with it when the lights went out.

With it, all sense of reason fled too. She would not be tied up like some animal and experimented on. Nor would she allow those in this room to leave it alive to do it to someone else.

In her heightened state of awareness, she could smell the wrongness of the Lycan-Z. They'd not been born this way but rather forced into this shape. No wonder Sascha wanted the females. Those with enough of the mutation he'd spoken of could temporarily reverse Lycanthropy. What she didn't understand was why he needed so many girls. It took Erryn just one bite when they were shifted to trigger the change from wolf to man.

Could it be her age made her ability more potent? If true, that had to be the real reason the Cabal banned pregnancies. Between that and too many alpha sons, they must have panicked.

At the same time, something didn't make sense. Why would a man who wanted to create Lycans need someone like Erryn who could reverse it? Unless...was it about control? Control the shift and he could blackmail alphas and even the Cabal. Especially if he created a delivery system that didn't require a bite.

She thought all this as her head swiveled left and right, testing the darkness. Scouting out the heartbeats. One, two, three wrong kind, a fluttery one that left her trembling. The last one was of the human. The so-called doctor, her primary target until he yelled, "Distract her. Kill the child if you must."

No.

Not the little girl. Despite wanting to rip his head from his shoulders, she had to protect the girl.

She barreled for the tiny heartbeat, knowing she had to make a stand. She arrived in time to grab the hairy arm reaching to rip out a vulnerable throat. She tore into the mutation, the bite leaving her with a sour taste in her mouth. Their blood was just wrong.

It took but a moment to finish her kill, and then the next tried to attack the child, following their last order. Annoying. She tore it apart, just like she eviscerated the third.

By the time she finished, only the little heartbeat

remained. What to do? The child needed her, but what of Sascha?

The decision was taken from her when Quinn arrived along with Gunner holding aloft a light.

Don't let him see.

She couldn't bear for him to think her a monster. He'd come to mean a bit more than just casual sex. When had that happened?

She fled by slamming into the wall, sensing the hollowness on the other side. The drywall shattered, and the plywood covering the hole in the stone wall of the castle exploded like toothpicks before her fury.

She emerged with a snarl as she spotted Sascha, still within reach if she could stop him from getting into the running car. He couldn't be allowed to escape because if he did, he'd only start over again. It stopped here and now.

Long strides and a leap with her powerful legs had her within arm's reach. She snared him and lifted, shaking the bastard, wanting answers before she killed him.

Such as, what had he'd done? Where did he keep his research? And who else knew? Because nothing of his legacy could survive.

The arrogant doctor didn't show fear as he spat, "Unhand me, bitch!"

"Not until you tell me everything," she hissed.

Surprise widened his eyes. "You can speak."

"So can you," she taunted, giving him another little shake. "And you're going to sing like a canary if you don't want me to literally shove your head where the sun don't shine."

His lips twisted. "You don't scare me. Take her!" he yelled.

Rather than move, she kept her stare on Sascha and let her innate senses guide her. Movement to her left had her shoving Sascha, growling, "Call them off or you die like your pets inside."

Rather than reply, or call off his guard dogs, noise from the castle swiveled their heads. She hissed as recognition hit.

Quinn.

Oh god. He'd seen her monster and, worse, recognized it as her given his lips moved, "Doc."

He'll hate me.

Or kill me.

She wasn't sure which would be worse.

She dropped Sascha and backed away.

Quinn opened his mouth, but before he could speak, Gunner strode forward. "Fuck me, you betrayed us too, Sascha? How many villagers did you rope into this mess?"

"Enough you never even suspected." The village doctor's lips twisted. "And the best is yet to come. I see you've brought an old friend. Hello, Frederick."

Fred? He'd come to her rescue too? She caught sight of her mentor stepping out last.

"Don't you hello me, asshole. I killed you." A visibly shaken Fred held himself tall.

"Tried," Sascha corrected. "And failed."

Wait, this was the man who'd tortured Fred? He'd never spoken much other than to say he'd almost died.

And she'd let go. Well, time to fix that mistake. Erryn lunged, with an open mouth as if she meant to eat him whole.

Sascha danced out of reach, squeaking, "Don't you fucking dare."

"Everyone freeze or I shoot." A woman dressed in a long woolen coat and holding a revolver emerged from the castle, the barrel pointed at the head of the little girl she carried. It was the child who'd been strapped to the gurney inside.

"Joella, you're in on it too?" Gunner appeared ready to cry. "You're supposed to be a village leader."

"Sascha is my brother. How could I say no?"

Erryn couldn't keep quiet despite knowing it would shock Quinn. Would he cringe hearing her lower, wolfish voice? "He's been manipulating the villagers. Encouraging pregnancies so he can steal the children."

"As if you can talk. Dr. Silver, I hear you did an experiment of your own with a pregnancy. Given your studies, I told Dmitri it was only a matter of time before you stumbled upon us." Joella eased down the steps with the child tucked against her and the gun still threatening.

The name Dmitri actually brought a gasp to Erryn's lips.

It turned an already pale Fred ashen. He held up

hands, trying to appear benign as he addressed Joella. "Hello, I don't know if you recall, but we met years ago. At a dinner with your husband, Dmitri." In an aside to Quinn and Gunner, Fred added, "He's Cabal. Longer than me by almost a decade."

"I thought the Cabal didn't have jurisdiction in this place," Quinn exclaimed.

An ashen Gunner exclaimed, "We didn't know he was Cabal."

"I suspect there will be an empty spot to fill after tonight." Joella shot a sly sneer in Fred's direction. "And I know just the person to fill it."

"You won't get away with this, Joella. You, Sascha, and Dmitri have gone too far."

"Ironic, coming from you, I have to say. I know your dirty secret, Frederick. And if you want to keep it, then you tell that little bitch to get on her knees."

"Tell me yourself, traitor," Erryn snarled.

Joella angled the gun against the child's temple and offered a cold, "Shall I shoot so she dies quick or slow?"

The child's salvation came in Sascha's smug form as he said, "Actually, I'd prefer to keep both of them for my studies. Shoot one of the males if you must. And might I say, good timing, sister."

"Figured you might be in trouble when I saw they found the tunnel in the clinic basement. Now, who am I shooting?" Joella still held the child and hadn't eased her grip on the gun. She angled it between Quinn and Fred as if knowing which two mattered most to Erryn.

She had no choice. Her knees hit the ground, and Quinn yelled, "No!"

Bang. He reeled and fell as she gasped and half rose.

"Shall I shoot your father next?" Joella re-aimed at Fred and smirked.

"What did you say?" Erryn's faint reply as she sank back down.

"Imagine my surprise when I did some digging on Frederick's nosy assistant. I could bore you with the little things he's done to help you since birth, but how about I skip to the end? Frederick is your father," Joella announced with a flourish.

"No he isn't," Erryn rebutted. "I ran the DNA myself." She'd done it with every single sample she took in a faint hope of finding out how she existed.

The sad expression on Fred's face went with his words. "I had no choice but to swap out the results. It was the only way I knew how to protect you."

The news rocked Erryn, and she howled before lunging, not for Sascha—as they probably expected—but the little girl. She ripped her from Joella and tossed her to Gunner but not in time to avoid the searing heat from a bullet that furrowed her arm.

Joella should have aimed better. Erryn lunged for her and ripped the gun from her hands.

The woman finally lost her cocky smile, and as fear oozed, pleasing Erryn immensely, she prepared to end the woman, only to be distracted as a vehicle arrived. A large SUV that spilled people with guns.

Suddenly revenge didn't matter as much as living. Lucky for her, Sascha kept screaming he wanted her alive, meaning the reinforcements weren't shooting to kill. Wouldn't have mattered even if they were.

Rage and the need to protect controlled her actions. She rushed the gunmen and got close enough to show them what a real monster was capable of. It involved much blood, spraying everything in its path as she ripped into the threat.

Two tried to run. There was something demoralizing, apparently, when she tore off someone's arm and used it to club the others. It added that extra element of horror to an already bloody situation.

The castle disgorged a few more enemies to make things even more chaotic. But after a few bursts of rapid gunfire, the shooting stopped, and as she licked blood from her lips, she realized they might have even won.

Bodies lay all over. Standing? Her and Fred, albeit wounded. Quinn, also shot, but looking fierce. Gunner was around the corner with the child.

The good guys had prevailed. Alas, the bad guys didn't exactly lose the day. A single vehicle raced away from the scene, the noise of its engine already fading. She had a feeling she knew who scurried away like a rat.

With the battle done, it left her unable to avoid those who remained. Especially Quinn.

What must he think of her? She couldn't tell what

the look on his face meant. Probably disgust because he saw her as a monster.

She'd always known things between them wouldn't end well. Rather than accept or face it, she ran.

17

WHAT THE FUCK had just happened?

Quinn couldn't help but try and figure out how the fuck they'd survived. Things appeared rather dire, hence why he'd used his gunshot to play possum so he could provide a surprise later.

But his contribution—distracting the castle guards —paled to the savage grace that was Doc. Where the wolfmen he'd met were true smelly beasts, she was beauty in motion with a scent that attracted. She didn't shy from the pain of her wounds but seemed to get stronger as she fought. Fought valiantly and prevailed, yet in the aftermath, she ran.

"Where is she going?"

"To hide until she gains control again." Rick's sobering answer.

"I'll follow her."

"You might not want to do that. She can be unpredictable in this shape."

"She shouldn't be alone," he insisted.

"She'd prefer no one see her in this state."

He hated that she fled because she feared their reactions. After all, Gunner and even Quinn had started out calling the hybrid shape a monster. How to tell her he didn't care and loved her all the same?

Wait, love?

"Fuck me, I can't believe I just saw your mate tear the arm off a man and slap him with it." Gunner sounded incredulous and admiring as he neared with the child tucked against him. She'd been in danger because they'd left her in that room. What they thought provided more safety didn't. They wouldn't make that mistake again.

Rick grimaced. "Ryn is very strong in her shifted body. And protective. Once she saw us in danger, it would have taken more than a few bullet holes to stop her."

"Guess you'd know since you're her dad," Quinn remarked sourly. He'd seen Erryn's shock at the news.

Rick's head dropped. "She doesn't seem too happy about it."

"Maybe 'cause you lied about it," Gunner drawled, having shifted the child so her head rested on his shoulder.

"I had no choice. The Cabal would kill her if they knew what she could do."

"A woman who can shapeshift. Not that big of a deal." Quinn didn't see the problem.

"When shifted, her bite reverses the change." Rick dropped the bombshell.

"Permanently?" Gunner huffed, sounding too hopeful.

Rick shook his head. "Not that we know of, but then again, she's not done much research. I discouraged it lest the wrong sort find out."

"And by wrong sort you mean Sascha." Talk about a convoluted story. Quinn rubbed a hand through his hair. "I don't like the idea of her being out there by herself."

"She can handle herself."

"It's not about that. I just don't want her to be alone." Quinn eyed Gunner. "You good, brother?"

"Go. Find her."

He nodded and had begun striding in the direction she'd fled when Rick added, "Tell her I'll explain everything when she returns."

"To the village," Gunner added. "Because this place is getting burnt to the ground."

True to his word, Gunner did set a fire that Quinn could smell as he followed the path Erryn left behind.

He didn't run. With her state of mind, he needed to be alert. She'd run out of steam eventually.

Or would she?

The woods weren't as quiet at night as people expected. Chipmunks could sound like a bear coming through the brush. Even the slightest breeze rattled branches and leaves.

Her path led to a stream, and he entered it, letting

the biting chill run over his ankles and feet. Instinct more than anything told him when to exit the water. She appeared to be going in an arc that would eventually bring her back to town. She kept a good pace for longer than he would have guessed.

When she crashed, she chose a place that provided a bit of a shield. Quietly, he sat cross-legged in front of her. A guard to her healing sleep. He remained alert the whole night, keeping watch over her curled form until the dawn brightened and kissed the skin of her exposed cheek.

She stretched and yawned before opening her eyes and seeing him.

She blinked.

He cocked his head. "What's up, Doc?"

She gave him the middle finger. "You shouldn't have followed me."

"I thought we were sleeping together these days."

"Stop trying to be cute. It's failing," she grumbled. "You don't have to be nice to me. Just kill me and get it over with."

"Are you fucking nuts?" His eyes widened. "I am not killing you. How can you even say that to me?" The indignation very real.

"We both know the Cabal would prefer I not exist."

"Funny, because Rick is doing everything he can to keep you safe."

"Because he's my father. It explains so much." She sighed.

"He told me that he'll tell you about it when we get back."

"We?"

"Yeah, we. We're a team."

"I accomplished what I set out to find. Lycan babies exist."

"Yup, and you'll need time to study what that means from a safe place. I'm thinking we should go somewhere tropical, but not on the beach. Too touristy. Maybe a tree house in a jungle?"

"I don't know, sounds too hot for me."

"Then you choose. I'll gladly follow."

"Why?" she asked, sitting up from the hollow, her hair a tangled mess, her clothes beyond a rag state. And yet she seemed so beautiful to him.

He reached to cup her chin and drew near. "Because I love you, Doc."

"Pretty sure I've got a pill to change your mind about that."

He snorted. "Ain't nothing that will cure me but you."

"Pity we don't have a bed," she murmured, closing the gap between their lips.

"For a smart girl, you ain't thinking." He cradled the back of her head to fully kiss her, the slide of their mouths steamy and passionate.

Somehow, they were standing, her body pressed against his, their mouths still locked. His hands roamed her flesh, thumbing gently over the still healing wounds already scarring over. "Tell me to stop," he murmured.

"Don't," she whispered back. "Don't let me go."

He crushed her to him, the connection between them tenuous but getting stronger. He'd make sure of it. She shoved at his pants, releasing him to her hand. Her strokes of his shaft had him thrusting his hips and groaning. He proved clumsy with her garments, the button popping before he could push them down and cup her.

Wet honey slicked his fingers. She sighed into his mouth and almost made him come when she said, "You picking me up, or am I bending over?"

He almost died of indecision. She chose for them, turning around and wiggling her bare ass at him. She bent over and grabbed the tree. Braced and ready.

He couldn't resist the temptation. The tip of his cock parted her nether lips. Slid in. Filled her and squeezed him.

Too good. He moved carefully lest he come too fast.

But she didn't want slow. Her hips rolled and pushed against him. With one hand, he grabbed hold of her hip. The other went under to fondle her clit, which tightened her around him, drawing a guttural sound.

"Oh fuck. Yes." He panted, needing her to come first. But damn he was so close.

She made a noise, a pleasure one, as his dick thrust in, and he lost it. His cock pulsed and spilled, and then it got totally squeezed as she joined him. Her climax rolled him into a second one that had him almost passing out.

Blame the lack of oxygen for him gasping, "Fuck, I love you."

She stiffened.

And for a second he thought he'd majorly screwed up. But then she relaxed and said, "Despite all the reasons I shouldn't, I love you too. However, if you maul me on the full moon because I smell too delicious, I will hamstring your ass."

"Good because I wouldn't want to live if I hurt you."

EPILOGUE

WHEN THEY EVENTUALLY MADE IT to the village, it was to a bit of chaos. A car went whipping past, piled inside with items. Other people still packed their cars.

Erryn wanted nothing more than a hot bath, food, and bed, yet she had to know. "Why are they leaving?"

A few reasons as it turned out. First there were the families of the traitors. People weren't taking revenge yet, but as the truth set in, that would change. Others didn't feel safe anymore. A town for Lycans working against Lycans? Because everyone knew. Joella hadn't been the only person to find the open door in the basement.

Velma recovered her emaciated granddaughter in a cell. Another family recovered a daughter as well. But the rest only received closure that their loved one had indeed died.

It was Gunner who offered them the news as he met them on the edge of town.

"And the little girl?" Erryn asked, feeling self-conscious in her filthy clothes.

"Back with her mom. And your dad is at the church waiting for you."

A conversation with him almost lost to the bath. Quinn remained steady at her side as she chose answers.

The moment she entered, Fred turned, and she could have kicked herself. How many times had she seen those eyes and that nose in the mirror?

Rather than launch into recriminations, she demanded replies. "Why did you impregnate my mother?"

"I wish I could say because I loved her, but ours was always only going to be a fleeting thing. To say she surprised me when she told me the news would be an understatement, given I'd had a vasectomy." His lips quirked.

"It failed?" She couldn't help a questioning lilt.

"More like I was misled, which turned into your mother getting pregnant. It killed me to tell her she couldn't keep the fetus. She didn't take it well."

While knowing it was coming, it still hurt. Quinn squeezed her hand. "You wanted her to abort me."

"To save her life," he insisted.

The doctor part of her understood. The rest... would eventually come to grips. "She obviously didn't listen, so what happened? How did she survive? Did you help her?"

"Not exactly. When she freaked, and refused the

219

abortion, I told her the truth, thinking she'd understand."

"You told her you were Lycan?"

"Yeah. She, of course, demanded proof. I am alpha. Changing is easy for me. When she saw I didn't lie, she asked for a night to process and give me answer. When a few days passed without word, I went knocking on her door to find her gone. I couldn't blame her wanting to escape me. I assumed she died until I saw you in my classroom. Not only are you the spitting image of her, she named you after her mother."

"You think she found out about the wolfsbane?" Erryn asked.

"She always was smart."

"While I can handle the fact you let her be alone after she ran from you, why didn't you tell me anything once I started working for you?" She couldn't quite stifle the hurt and anger.

"I wanted to tell you, but I worried about the danger it would put you in if anyone found out. I've seen what you can do."

"And Sascha knows it now as well." If only she'd killed him rather than tried to get answers.

"He's an evil man. He's the one who intentionally botched my vasectomy. He was the one who performed it, although, at the time, he bore a different name. The Cabal recruited him when the bite failed to work. Given his medical degree, they shuffled him around as a mobile neutering unit. Only it turned out he wanted people to get pregnant. Wanted the aborted fetuses for science he said." His lips turned down.

"He was experimenting on people under the guise of working for the Cabal." Quinn whistled. "That had to piss them off."

"I was the one sent to eliminate him, only he turned the tables and captured me. For years I was his test subject until I escaped with some help." He glanced at Quinn and Gunner. Both men ducked as if embarrassed. "Once I recovered, I set out to kill him, and thought I succeeded given I'd tossed his bleeding body into a river. Apparently, I should have taken off his head to be sure."

"Where is Sascha?" she asked. She didn't recall seeing his body.

"Escaped with his sister," a disgusted Gunner replied. "And no one is interested in looking. They're all scattering."

"Can you blame them?" she stated. "Packs are supposed to be havens for Lycans and their families."

"Gherdeal wasn't a pack," Gunner reminded.

"Exactly my point. These people need to feel safe."

"Speaking of safe..." Rick ducked his head. "It would appear Joella and her husband, Dmitri, have complicated matters by telling the Cabal you're my daughter. As a result, they've requested we both come in for questioning."

"Brazen considering their crimes," Gunner noted.

"Not if they're working with other Cabal members," Rick noted.

Quinn pinched his lips. "It's a trap."

"Most likely which is why you need to find a place to hide with Ryn. As do I until the traitors within the Cabal are dealt with."

"Go where, though?" Erryn asked.

"Anywhere you like. Just name the place, doc."

She chose the Alps. Cold outside, but cozy in front of the fireplace with her werewolf bodyguard.

MEANWHILE, *back in the UK...*

The car had been cleaned of monster blood. The leather shone. The carpets were like new.

Brock had worked his ass off bringing the car back to its pristine condition rather than deal with her highness, princess pain in his ass. A vampire didn't have the right to be as hot as her.

Attraction should have been easy to fight. Tell that to his dick every time Arianna came around. Must be some kind of vampy pheromone thing—and that sweet ass of hers. Heart-shaped and perfect.

But it was her mouth and her rapier wit that enthralled him most, so when Arianna came around, looking hot as ever, wearing that damnable mask he wanted to tear off, and snapped, "I'm going into the sewer hunting monsters. You in?"

He stupidly said, "Hell, yeah.

LOOKS LIKE WE'RE NOT DONE WITH OUR BIG

CITY LYCANS. WILL BROCK FIND LOVE IN WERE-WOLF'S PRINCESS? AND WHAT ABOUT A SECOND CHANCE FOR GUNNER IN WEREWOLF NOEL?

For more books and fun see EveLanglais.com

CPSIA information can be obtained
at www.ICGtesting.com
Printed in the USA
BVHW031748030723
666734BV00006B/153